KRISTOPHER LIOUDIS AND VALERIE LIOUDIS

Breakdown

Aftershock Zombie Series Book Two

INSULT TO THE
WRITTEN WORD
PUBLISHING

First edition

ISBN: 978-1-62676-735-5

This book was professionally typeset on Reedsy.
Find out more at reedsy.com

Contents

A Quick Recap

To the reader:

I highly recommend that you read Book One in the Aftershock Zombie Series before you begin this book. But, just in case you can't, won't or need a refresher if you have, here is a breakdown of the story and characters from book one.

First, the story:

Aftershock begins with the zombie outbreak. There is no big government explanation or news story to tell those not shambling around searching for brains to devour what has happened and what to do. They are left on their own to find safety and supplies. Everything in the system has collapsed, and each person has to come to grips that help is not on the way.

What they do have is a mysterious flyer that fell down from the sky. On it, there is the promise of a sanctuary and a map leading them to New Jersey of all places. Each group needs to decide if they are willing to risk it all to head off to an unknown destination that could be more dangerous than the undead monsters they will have to face to get there.

Some of the characters have a secret that may be the way to save what is left of humanity. A few of them are immune to the zombie outbreak. They only know this because they have been bitten, but didn't turn. No one knows what caused the outbreak in the first place, so knowing why someone is immune is out of the question. Many of them haven't shared this information with anyone yet out of fear.

Characters from Aftershock whose stories continue in Breakdown:

Daniel: Foul mouthed and angry at the world, Daniel was a grunt in the Army when the zombies showed up. His commanding officer had sent him alone into a barn in what Daniel would describe as a suicide mission. He was abandoned by his unit, left with a bite on his leg and shit in his pants. Eventually he ended up with Reverend Mathis and his group. The Reverend wanted Daniel to take a leadership role, but Daniel had no interest in it.

Amy: At the start of the outbreak Amy finds her brother eating her sister-in-law in front of his three children Garett (16), Zoe (12) and Hannah (5). She suddenly becomes the adult in charge of three kids in the midst of the zombie apocalypse. She realized how important her role was when she was bitten by a zombie, as she assumed the children would be left alone. But that wasn't the case, as she was immune and recovered from the bite. The small group walled themselves up in her house until the flyers end up in their reach and they decide to head towards NJ. She finds Mick in an abandoned town, and he joins their small group. Amy watches in horror as Hannah is killed by a truck in a place she had hoped would be their new home. Soon after, they meet a group of preppers that are headed towards NJ, too. Garett befriends a girl his age, Emma, who they "adopt" into their small family after her father is killed during a supply run.

William: Most people would be traumatized seeing their parents die in front of them. Not William. His calm, detached nature allows him to look at the world through a different set of eyes. Where others saw zombies devouring the living, he saw people invading others' personal space. When he teams up with Ian, he is eager to learn how to be a good soldier just like his friend. His attention to detail and literal interpretation of directions makes him a fast learner. Ian feels a sense of duty to protect William, but at twenty-four years old, William wants to be self-sufficient. That can be difficult when those around you see you as disabled.

Ian: Locked away in some secret government lab, Ian's immunity was being tested by doctors who refused to treat him better than a slab on the table. The outbreak ripped through the building leaving Ian on his own to escape and head as far away from his now deceased or undead captors. Lucky for him, all his years of military training gave him a leg up on being prepared for the chaos he would muck through on his way to NJ. He was alone until he found William fending for himself without really understanding the danger he was in. Aftershock ends with the two of them reaching the sanctuary on the flyer.

Wayne: Wayne's story starts with him locked with his family in an underground bunker. He spends his time connecting with other preppers on his HAM radio. As much as he hates to admit it, he realizes along with the other preppers that they can't just ride this one out underground. Those that are close enough to get to the sanctuary in NJ meet up and make a caravan together towards the destination on the flyer. Wayne is the leader of the group without ever really being given the power or title. Every day they let a new member lead the way, but in the end, the large decisions land on his lap. He feels trapped by the responsibility.

Reverend Mathis: A Methodist Pastor, Reverend Mathis was in his church when the zombies came. First, the humans attacked him and his wife. They desecrated his church with their actions, killed her, and left him for dead. His faith was broken, but a group in need brought him back to the warm embrace of God's love. Just as he grew his flock, Daniel arrived like an answer from the Lord All Mighty to a prayer for help keeping them safe. His interactions with Daniel have been a test of faith, though, as his resistance to the Lord's call has caused a rift between them. Daniel went so far as to beat the Reverend to a bloody pulp, but forgiveness is the Pastor's nature, and he holds no grudge.

Max and Rocky: Just a good ole farm boy and his dog, Max and Rocky are an unlikely duo to survive long term in the zombie apocalypse. Max found out he was immune to the zombie outbreak when a friend took a bite out of him and his parents spent days waiting for him to die. He miraculously survived, but when his mother was bitten, she was not immune and his father shot her. Just a short while into Max's journey with his father towards NJ, the nine-year-old had to shoot his father when he was infected, too. This left Max and Rocky on their own. They spent some time with Daniel, the Reverend, and their group, but left due to their constant bickering. At the end of Aftershock, Max and Rocky are on their own and unsure of where they will go next.

Mick: Before the outbreak, Mick was a bit of a dead-beat. He was divorced with two children that no longer had any interest in talking to him. His days were spent going to work, then the bar. Rinse. Repeat. The plant shut down as the world fell apart, and Mick and his buddies were left keeping seats warm at the local dive. That all changed when they were attacked there, and Mick escaped with a bite that he was somehow immune to. Amy found him after he had run out of booze and smokes. Before her, his plans never stretched more than his next drag or drink. He quickly fell hard for the woman and her family, and became the protector of their group.

Vincent: A commercial fisherman off of Long Beach Island,NJ. Vincent and the crew of his ship were at sea when the outbreak occurred. One of the crew brought the sickness with them when they went out on what would be their last trip. Vincent had to fight to stay alive as his fellow shipmates went down one by one. In the end only Earl and himself made it back to land, but not before one of the zombies bit Vincent. Once he discovered his immunity, he decided God chose him to start the new human race, and he began the search for a suitable queen. Jessica, a famous author, had the misfortune of being in his kingdom, and proving she was immune, too. She escaped with the help of one of Vincent's men, and a well timed breach of their defenses. He had be holding her hostage, and forcing her to attempt to repopulate the Earth with him. Earl, now Vincent's second in command, will be the only one left that will be in between Vincent and his violent tendencies towards his subjects.

I

Breakdown

A Continuation of Aftershock.

1

Ian

William and I did our time in quarantine. It wasn't half bad. For three whole nights I could sleep relatively soundly and the food was gourmet compared to all the garbage William and I had been eating.

You could do a lot worse for a bunkmate than William. He fascinated the shit out of me. His take on everything was pure logic. And he was smart as hell, too. He had memorized his Chain of Command from the C.I.C. all the way down to me (I was honored to make the list) and he could talk through every single step of breaking down an M4, which can be hard to do without one in your hands.

One night, while we were just shooting the shit, I asked William about the scar on the top of his head. It was pretty gnarly even though the hair around it had grown in and covered most of it up. He told me that a neighbor had tried to kiss him there. I didn't get it at first, but as the story went on, it started to clear up. He went on for about five minutes, relaying the story of what had to be his mother's death with zero emotion, which was creepy in and of itself, but when he got to the part about the kiss, I about jumped out of my bunk. From the way he described it, almost like he wasn't even involved, just reading it out of a newspaper, it all but had to be that he was bitten. And that meant he was immune like me.

I hadn't told anyone about my little mishap, not sure about what the reaction would be, but if I survived a bite and William survived a bite… There had to be others. I know that's why they kept me at the hospital in Virginia instead of just capping me and throwing my corpse in the furnace. I had to wonder how many others there were out there immune to whatever the hell this was.

I decided to keep this information under my hat, figuring it better to wait until I could make more sense of what it meant. Besides, this was back when I still didn't know if we were really being held in quarantine, or just being held captive.

After we passed the three-day mark, we were let out to meet the rest of the group. Mike explained that this was really just a waystation and that most of the survivors they were harboring were holed up at an airport about 20 or so miles away. He said William and I would have to visit there at some point and make the introductions to the rest of the leadership committee. He had already told about them about us via their daily radio communications. Apparently, anybody with a useful skill was given, well, not "special" treatment, but maybe a little more attention. My military experience was apparently a commodity.

The Major wasn't kidding about this place being in the middle of nowhere. It seemed about as far into the sticks as you could get in this state. Mike called it the Pine Barrens. And to think, I'd always figured New Jersey was all factories and toxic waste…

Mike gave us the rundown as William and I ate breakfast our first morning out of quarantine. We were given plates of smoked deer meat, some kind of rough bread and real, honest-to-goodness eggs. Like I said, gourmet after canned goods and vending machine garbage.

"This place used to be one of those historic village-type places," Mike began, "You know what I'm talking about? The kind of place they would take school trips to and tell the kiddies about what life was like in olden days. Well, this place was an iron works about 200 years ago. There's still an awful lot of bog ore out there in the river. Anyway, there's the old bunk houses that you've already seen, the mill, the main house, what's left of the forge... Lots of old buildings with good heavy walls."

"That's great and all," I said, "but where did you get the eggs?"

"Chicken coops," Mike said, pointing over my shoulder at twin rows of low, wooden huts. I did, in fact, hear the clucking from within and couldn't help but feel a little like an idiot.

After breakfast, Mike continued the tour. They had some makeshift radio equipment, CB and HAM, in the mansion and had maintained communications with the airport and even a few other small groups in the area. Comms with those groups had become more sporadic the longer this all dragged out. Like maybe those people kept thinking somebody was going to come and save them, right up until the dead were at their door. Mike said they had scout groups out most of the time, collecting resources, looking for survivors, keeping tabs on a group to the north the was getting sizeable, but keeping mostly to themselves.

I was more than a little impressed with the work they had done. Wrecked cars were piled at the two road entrances. Fortified ranch fence ran almost the entire perimeter and tripwires had been set through the gaps. Mike explained that the alarms were all silent, which I thought was smart. Any kind of noise seemed to bring those bastards out of the woodwork in droves.

As if on cue, a little, red light flashed on the side of his radio.

"South fence again." He shook his head and called to some of the men. "You may as well come along. It's the next stop on the tour anyway."

I motioned for William to follow me as we took off toward the point of contact, but he was already in tow, weapon in hand, that same steady, matter-of-fact look on his face. We headed out on foot into the woods to the south. A group of about a dozen zombies had tripped one of the alarms at the perimeter and had gotten themselves tangled in the barbed wire strung there. One had nearly succeeded in freeing itself by ripping off most of one its legs down to the bone.

Mike leaned close to me and said, "This isn't the largest group we've seen in a while. Though it is starting to thin out around here."

I nodded an affirmative and leveled my weapon at the one closest to me.

Mike shook his head, "Too much noise. Don't know how many more are out there." He turned to the rest of the group that had gathered, "Fix bayonets."

The group did so and moved in to deal with the undead. It looked like they had practiced this maneuver a hundred times. Shit, for all I knew, they probably had. Mike pointed to me, William, and three others to go out past the wire line. "Move out one kilometer in a straight line then sweep your way back. They move in packs. If there are any stragglers out there I want them dealt with, but quietly. We don't leave these things alive."

We headed out into the woods and moved slowly into the trees. Even as we passed out of sight of the fence, I saw several of the group that stayed behind begin to police up the area. They had put on heavy leather gloves, the kind linemen used to handle high tension wires, and were pulling the bodies out of the snarls of wire. By the time we had made it out to one-click marker, I could smell the bodies burning. It still kind of reminded me of roast pork.

We spread out a little and proceeded to work our way back to the compound moving slowly in a swaying arc. One of the guys found signs that some zombies had been through, and by that, I mean he found chunks of flesh that had scraped off onto the jagged stump of a fallen tree. We made it back to the fence without any additional contact. Cleanup efforts there had just completed, the smoldering remains of our uninvited guests lay in a pile. Two men remained behind to make sure the pyre didn't start a forest fire and the rest of us headed back toward the main house.

Outside the back entrance to what had been a mansion a hundred and fifty years ago and was now central command, we stripped off our dirty fatigues and washed up.

William asked Mike, intent on calling him "Sir" even though Mike had told him it wasn't necessary, how many zombies he had killed. There wasn't any wonder or even curiosity on his face, just that same calculating look he got when he was training with his weapon or washing his hands or figuring out whether to eat the bread or the meat first at dinner.

"Don't really keep track, kid. I would say…" He scratched his chin affecting a thoughtful pose, "Somewhere between fifty and ten thousand."

I chuckled a little as William pooched out his bottom lip

and nodded. He was a great mimic for facial expression, but I knew he was only aping what he'd seen others do. Mike's answer seemed to sate him though and he went back to digging through the pile of clean clothes trying to find a pair of pants in his size.

Mike turned to me, "You two will likely be headed over to the airport tomorrow. You'll be introduced to command there and then they'll figure out what to do with you. Everybody gets a job. I've already talked to them about both of you. Could be you'll end up back here with me guarding the quarantine. Can't say that would upset me. I kind of like you two and we can always use more people around that know how to handle themselves. They're busy over there, too. The area was more densely populated so there's more attention, but then again, we're the ones broadcasting our location."

We headed inside where Mike showed us a map of the surrounding area. Almost the entire map was shaded green with wide swatches of blue, state forests, lakes, and rivers. That explained the low population density as compared to other parts of the northeast.

Mike pointed to a few areas of interest. "This used to be an Air Force bombing range to the north of where we are now. Civilian population centers prior to the invasion, or whatever the fuck it was, were here, here, here, and here. There are also two nuclear power plants within 100 kilometers, one to the north and one to the west. We have a guy over at the compound that worked at Oyster Creek. He swears they shut the plant down before everyone bugged out, but we have no way of knowing about Hope Creek. We do know that another plant to the south caught fire, but since we're not glowing in the dark, I'm guessing it was either coal or gas. Must have been a big one, we could see the plume of smoke from here. In between, miles and miles and miles of pine forest."

Mike said they would fill me in on the rest of what I needed to know tomorrow and went up to his room. William and I returned to our bunk house and gathered together our gear.

"Will we be taking the truck?" William asked.

"Don't know William. I want to trust these people, but it may be better to keep a few secrets just now."

"Like how you were bitten?"

I turned on my heel surprised. I glanced around to see if anyone was within ear shot. Had they been, there would have been a lot of explanation required. We were relatively alone. One of the guys from the fence wandered by across the dirt road and waved. Had he heard something, I'm pretty sure he would have reacted.

I hustled William back to the bunkhouse and practically dragged him up the stairs.

"How did you know about my bite?"

He scratched his chin, mimicking Mike's gesture from earlier, "I saw the scar a long time ago. It looks like teeth marks, but not like a dog's or a cat's teeth, like people teeth. It just makes sense. I think my mother was bitten by someone too. I don't think she got a scar from it though. She is dead and dead people don't get scars."

I was impressed, but not surprised, by his deductive skills. Anybody that looked at the world as logically as he did could have figured it out. I had done a decent job of hiding the scar from most people, when we were inspected during in-processing here, I explained it as a shrapnel wound from my time overseas. Nobody questioned it since I didn't turn into a walking corpse a day later. I was going to have to talk to someone about this, but who? I was still on the fence about this place. Mike was alright, I was sure of that, but what about these others at the airport? I didn't want William to be subjected the constant testing I had already gone through. He already got stared at enough for being a little strange. I kept explaining that he wasn't retarded, just different.

William snapped me from my musing, "We have to keep this a secret right?"

"At least for now," I replied.

"I do not like keeping secrets. I do not like to lie. Father says that telling lies is not proper."

"I know William, but for right now it might be dangerous for other people to know about us."

He looked at me, trying to mimic a quizzical look but falling just short, "Us?"

"I think you were bitten too. The scar on your head looks just like mine. Plus, I don't many people that kiss with their teeth. I have seen a lot of people get bitten by those things, you know the things I am talking about, right? Most of the time they die and come back, but you and I didn't. I don't know what that means, but until I figure it out we cannot tell anyone. Okay?"

He nodded thoughtfully, again falling just short of expressing the emotion he was trying to portray, "Okay. I will keep the secret."

And that was it. He was already on to the next topic of thought. "When will I resume training?"

"Maybe this afternoon if we have time. You did good this morning."

He looked genuinely pleased at that, not happy, but it seemed to register that I was paying him a compliment. I still couldn't get a grip on how his head worked. We spent the afternoon out in a field doing drill and ceremony. William enjoyed drill, I guess it appealed to his logic.

That night we ate a dinner of more smoked deer meat and tough bread. I told William to head back to the bunkhouse after we ate and that I would be there in a while. I wanted to talk to Mike. I gave a little more backstory on our trip up from Virginia, filling in some of the details about our ambush and the handful of run-ins we had with the undead.

Mike sat there nodding, and as if he knew what I was asking said, "They won't split the two of you up if you don't want to be. Bad for morale to go breaking up battle buddies. As long as he shows enough aptitude at whatever job you get assigned to, they'll let him tag along. Based on how he handled himself this morning, I don't see any trouble."

I thanked Mike for the encouragement and headed off to the bunk, I wanted to catalog what gear we had with us before heading out in the morning.

Driving in to the airport the next day, I half thought they were airlifting people out, but they had turned the place into one hell of a compound. The guy driving us in explained that the place had been a small airport with an airbase attached to it before the shit hit the fan. It already had a double row of 10-foot chain link topped with barbed wire and only two roads in. Over time, a large moat had been dug around the outer run of fence and K-rails had been stacked at the entrances. More than enough to stop vehicles and slow down anybody on foot. The airport itself was small, only four terminals. The tower provided a great view of the surrounding area. Our chauffer explained that in the first few months, while they were digging the moat and trenches, they'd seen a fair amount of action from both the living and the dead. They had successfully fended off all would-be invaders, but suffered more than their share of casualties.

Back when the chaos originally set in, the airport employees joined forces with the Air Force guys to secure the facility. Mike had been among their number and he later told me it was only because there were so many military guys around that they were able to get it done so quickly. It wasn't long before somebody had the idea to send out the two choppers, and even one of the 727's, with a flyer they Xeroxed in one of the admin offices. The goal was to put together enough of a force to defend the place and to bring in anybody seeking shelter. They decided to use Batsto as an intermediary locale after an infected refugee almost brought the whole thing down when he attacked the group he was staying with. It was also thought it might not be a good idea to broadcast their exact location.

At first, they would just swing by Batsto every couple days and see if anyone was there. Later on, it was set up as an actual command post and Mike was sent over to run the show.

They hadn't seen much activity in at least a few months before we showed up. For about the first six months, they saw a pretty steady inflow of people from the surrounding area, after that visitors tapered off but they still saw a trickle of newcomers. Once you made it through the quarantine period, you got carted over to the airport. There, you got a job and started pulling your weight, or you were asked politely to leave. There wasn't a whole lot of in-fighting among residents. Everybody seemed to understand that life inside the fence was a whole lot easier than life outside it. Funny how the Apocalypse can make you reevaluate how annoying you do or don't find other peoples' idiosyncrasies, especially when a simple fist fight can get you banished to a wasteland crawling with the living dead. Not that there weren't assholes, there were always assholes, it's just that if a guy can fix wiring or keep a genny running or knows how to build a solar still you can kind of look past the fact that he's a douche bag. And anybody that couldn't keep their shit in line was dealt with pretty quickly.

William and I were both assigned to guard duty. No surprise there, though they had originally intended to put William on trash removal and sanitation. I lobbied to keep him with me at Batsto. I was one of three people he would even talk to, let alone take orders from. And besides, I felt responsible for the kid and I wanted to keep him close. We spent our days patrolling the woodline, manning the tower in the big main house, and making sure petty squabbles didn't escalate into anything.

2

Jeremy

Reluctantly, I was part of a group of three. I found the two of them hiding in the woods on my way to the sanctuary in New Jersey. She was a leggy blonde whose roots had long since taken over. He was an angry meathead with too much in the muscle department and not enough in the brains. I would have walked right past them, but hiding him was almost impossible. I could have kept walking, but the look on her face screamed that she needed help. As pathetic as it seems, I am a sucker for a damsel in distress. Even if the damsel looks less like a princess, and more like a character from some shitty reality show.

There we were, a newly formed trio, wandering through unknown woods hoping to find shelter for the first time since meeting. He mostly grunted but she rattled on and on, her voice running over you like lotion on dry skin. All sex and no substance. He towered over us both, lumbering along with no purpose but tromping and stomping. About an hour into our trek, I discreetly popped in my earbuds and cranked the tunes for a while. I had the Walkman, yes, I said Walkman, shoved in my hidden jacket pocket.

Neither of my new buddies noticed the difference. He kept stomping, she kept chattering, and I kept smiling like a buffoon. Not much had changed for me since zombies took over the damn world. I still got told what to do, pushed around, and dismissed as the sidekick. Works for me. I've spent my whole life just floating along and letting others worry about the bullshit. Why should a few face eating monsters change that?

Right around sundown we spotted a hunting shack. There have been a few of these on my trip so far. Some are empty, some are not. This one looked completely abandoned and, for good measure, the last set of inhabitants had knocked out one of the walls. If we were going to set up here for the evening, we would have to pull something together quickly. Good thing we basically had an ox with us. He may not be that bright, but he could definitely be useful dragging logs around.

Her name was Crystal, and I knew without being told that in a prior life she had been a stripper. His name was Ben. I chuckled inwardly when he told me. His name could not be more fitting. So Big Ben, Lady Crystal, and I did our best to set up a secure camp for the night. I laid low, fixing the things I saw Ben leave undone, but never claiming credit for them. It was easier if no one looked to me for leadership. I was fully capable of taking care of myself but I had no interest in putting together some ragtag group to wander through the woods, fighting the undead as we go.

Ben was out the moment the work was done. That man had a snore that could have raised the dead straight out of their graves even before the zombie apocalypse allowed that to happen. Crystal looked at me with hungry eyes. Unattached women were hard to come by in our present state, so I considered it for a second. But my past experiences had taught me that this would be a bad idea.

Crystal may not have seen it, but Ben had claimed her as his own. Now, I may not agree with marking your territory like that and calling a woman yours, but I am also not dumb enough to think my sensibilities mattered squat against his brick sized fists. The first time I ever got laid was ruined by some brute chucking concrete garden decorations in a fit of jealous rage. Concrete garden goose littered the street and the commotion almost ruined what was a huge milestone in my life. Crystal was not the kind of woman who knew how to accept 'no' for an answer, however, so she persisted until I faked falling asleep.

She huffed and puffed for a bit, but eventually succumbed to her own exhaustion. With her finally asleep, I slid a log over to the makeshift wall and stared out in the distance. Back to the only real escape I had, I clicked the play button. Simple Man. How appropriate. I hummed along quietly and flashed back to the days before our lives so drastically changed. I missed the convenience of it all. It wasn't simpler, but it was easier. I missed that.

I had finally found a way to make a living off of one of the only things that had brought me joy. People make fun of karaoke, but there were thousands of bars across the country packing people in to sing their hearts out to their favorite songs. Most of those people were terrible, but not me. I had finally found my niche, and then it all disappeared. Not just my life, but everyone's lives.

All I had left was that Walkman and my few precious songs. It was all I needed though. There were two extremes at night when you were trying to relax, the first being the extreme silence, which was extremely unsettling. Then there was the

16

deafening sound of zombies, moaning and groaning as they shuffled closer and closer to your hiding spot. My music broke the silence and covered the noise. It was a comfort I thanked God for nightly.

They were getting closer as the night dragged on. My two travelling companions were oblivious and didn't even stir. Not so much as a flinch. Ben was part of the problem, with his obnoxious snoring. I tried everything to quiet his ass down but anything I did only delayed his log sawing for a minute at most. Crystal could sleep through both Ben's noise and the zombies. It was amazing, yet amazingly stupid. The more I hung around these two, the more surprised I was that they were still alive.

As time passes, the weak and stupid have been dropping like flies. The last group I stumbled upon had a couple of duds in it. Running low on ammo, they decided one day to raid a camp they had spotted. It may have worked if they had done even the smallest amount of recon, but instead the idiots went charging in and were shot down before they even hopped the fence. I knew it was a disaster waiting to happen, so I offered to stay back and guard the supplies with the only other sane group member, John.

We witnessed the massacre and then quickly packed up everything we could carry. John and I traveled together for two weeks until I woke up one morning and saw that he was gone. He took half of the supplies and headed out on his own. I wasn't upset when he left, though. It made sense. John had spent those two weeks going on and on about his family in New York. He probably decided he would rather go find them than spend any more time wandering around with me.

Problem is, without a destination, the whole thing seems kind of pointless. Ben and Crystal were looking for some place they found on the world's least likely invite. While scavenging in some random town, they found a paper with directions to a safe zone. As much as I like being on my own, a real compound sounds like a 5-star resort right about now. Ben and Crystal were lucky I showed up, too. With his brilliant map reading skills, they had spent a good two days heading in the wrong direction.

So now I'm sitting here, debating which of the two to wake up for watch. I guess I will go with Ben because I am too tired to play cat and mouse with Crystal. If I am going to stay with these two until we reach New Jersey, I am going to have to find a way to permanently discourage that woman from pursuing me. It would be a shame to avoid death by zombie only to end up worm food by ogre.

3

Ken

People are stupid. People have always been stupid. Always waiting until a problem is staring them directly in the face before deciding to do anything about it. Back when this whole zombie apocalypse thing.. God that sounds so stupid saying it out loud. Anyway, when this all started, in those first few weeks when we could have done something about it, people were too busy arguing with each other to realize that maybe we should hold off on the finger pointing and deal with the fact that dead people were getting up from autopsy tables and morgues and funeral homes and accident scenes and pretty much anywhere you might find a dead body and killing thousands more.

I remember it boggling my mind that people could have remained ignorant for so long. Within a month, there were cases throughout the US, all over Mexico and into southern Canada. The news would report an incident in a city and show footage of a convoy of military trucks rolling in. Three days later that city would be visible on the horizon as a plume of smoke if you were lucky enough to live within viewing distance. After a while, everybody lived close enough to watch a city burn, or to be in one that was already on fire.

It only took a couple months for the chaos to really set in. Once the first major cities began to burn, it was like an avalanche. People all over the country banded together to fight the undead hordes, and ended up feeding them in an unending wave of stupidity. As soon as people realized that the Government wasn't coming to their rescue, they chose one of two paths. They either tried to hide out in barricaded homes or took the opportunity to run wild in the streets.

I was flying home after a conference in New York on, of all things, infectious disease in the 21st Century, when they finally decided to shut down air travel. Maybe, had the government thought of closing interstate borders sooner, it might have made a difference. By the time travel was restricted, it was already too late. Nevertheless, all flights already en route were to be immediately grounded. That's how I ended up in Atlantic City. My flight from Newark tried sneak out under the wire, but apparently, the pilot received word that if he didn't land immediately, we would be shot down. So, we touched down in this po-dunk airport. The place was packed with stranded travelers. Every one of them angry at having been inconvenienced by the undead.

Of those of us stuck in the airport, some decided to go out on foot or in cars stolen from long-term parking. I can't tell you how most of them faired, for all I know they're safe and sound in some bunker somewhere. I do know that I saw more than a few of them come back days or weeks later, smashing themselves against the fence or stuck in the rows of barbed wire at the gate. Me? I'm glad I stayed. The decision was pretty much made for me. By the time I made it past the shock and the fear, there was no way I would have made it more than a day in what the outside world had become. I'm not saying I'm a coward, just not a hero. I was a research scientist in my other life. Epidemiological pharmacologists are not known for our combat prowess. Besides, I couldn't get a hold of my wife, which meant that she was either dead or in one of the safe zones that had been hastily set up, which probably also meant she was dead. Considering that she had told me before I left for the conference that she was filing for divorce, I figured this was a less messy method for dissolving the marriage. So, I stayed at the airport, eventually moving over to Batsto because it was quieter and there were fewer people.

The conference I was coming home from was held mainly to discuss the emergence of rapidly evolving viruses like the strains of influenza in China that changed so much from host to host that vaccination was totally ineffective. Reports from India last year talked about a strain of rabies that was threatening to become airborne. It was a bunch of backstabbing, nay-saying, and vying for government funds. Not one peep about what had sprung up in the weeks leading up to the conference.

On the fifth day of the conference, outside the convention hall, while some of the greatest minds in medicine invented problems to throw money at, there were people in the streets rioting. And dying, lots of them were dying, and then of course getting back up and killing others. A National Guard unit had to be assigned to escort us back to the airport. Thirty minutes after we were in the air, word came from the pilot that we would be making an unscheduled landing at Atlantic City International, but a few of us noticed the F-whatever fighter jet that "escorted" us down to the landing strip.

So now I sit here in this abandoned manager's office flipping through journals, my notebooks, some college anatomy textbook I found in someone's luggage and dragged over here with me. Anything I can get my hands on to try and continue what little progress we made before communication collapsed. All I have are theories with no real way to test them anyway. Like it matters. Even if I found the cause, what are the chances of developing a cure? And let's say for argument's sake, that by some fluke, I find the magic bullet. How the hell would we manufacture it? And deliver it? Even just to disseminate the information... We wasted most of the fuel sending the chopper and the smaller planes out to drop flyers. The helicopter was supposed to go all the way to Florida, but that was months ago and we haven't heard back from them. Mike says we have to keep a couple of the big 737's fueled as escape vehicles. Great idea, but where the hell would we go if the shit hit the fan here?

4

Amy

Mick and I had another one of our long talks about leaving the group. There came a point where we realized the decision to stay was based on the same mentality that keeps a woman in an abusive relationship, fear of the unknown rather than a real desire to be with them anymore. Fear drives so much of our behavior since zombies have become our main, and only, focus. We no longer have the luxury of a lazy Sunday spent curled up against the one we love. We'd try though, and take little moments while wrapped up in each other on some rooftop in some town we had never heard of before our trek towards New Jersey.

Mick was getting tired of following orders and I was tired of the monotony. Add to that the bite in the air at night, reminding us that it's time to find a place to settle for the winter. It wasn't safe to spend it on the road. None of us are really trained to know when a storm will roll through. We spent our lives depending on a man in a little box to tell us if we needed an umbrella and panicking if a few inches of snow were in the forecast. Yet, the preppers seemed content with just crawling along. Maybe the monotony is what they need, the safety in knowing each day will be like the last.

Wayne was the only other person who looked like he wanted to bolt. I think he stayed for a different reason than Mick and myself, though. His role had primarily been leading the group, even with the crazy system they cooked up where each person gets a turn at lead. The real decisions were always made by Wayne. He allowed the rest to feel like they had an equal say but, at the end of the day, it was all on him. That kind of responsibility was a chain that tethered him to the group.

"What if we can get Wayne to leave with us?" I whispered as I pushed my face into Mick's back and breathed in deeply. For a man who hadn't had a decent washing since all hell broke loose, he smelled wonderful. It was a deep, musky smell, not off putting like body odor, but masculine like men smelled before they began dousing themselves with body sprays.

"I don't know if we could ever convince him that everyone would be alright without him. If I don't believe it, why would he? I know most of these people know how to survive, but they don't have the people skills to maintain the group. They all need to stay together to stay alive. I just don't know if he would be able to do it. His conscious will probably stop him from leaving. "

"Well, we need to make our decision soon. Winter is coming and I don't want to be caught on the road for it. We're going to need time to set up camp."

"The zombies seem to move slower as it gets colder, maybe they'll freeze up for the winter," he pondered.

"Guess we'll find out soon," I sighed.

Gently kissing his back one more time, I rolled over and started lacing my boots. Somewhere along the way I had morphed into a character from a post-apocalyptic video game. Black boots, black pants and a black t-shirt had become my uniform. It's a survival thing. Color makes you stand out, and standing out is the last thing you want. I had a shitty black windbreaker, but I needed to make it a priority to find our small family better cold weather clothes over the next few days. The preppers had started rubbing off on me, and, annoying as they may be, I gained some good habits when it comes to preparedness.

I unzipped the tent and stretched my way onto the roof. Half of the group was awake and already working. Mick and I had managed to fall into the routine of never being first or last to wake. I wandered over to the far corner of the roof and tapped Garett on the shoulder. He had been on watch for the last portion of the night. He turned towards me, and stared at me with eyes that were far too serious for a boy of his age.

I keep saying 'boy', but I know damn well that he's not a child. Both Zoe and Garett have had birthdays in the last month. I did my best to celebrate with each of them. I found Zoe a new backpack and a fancy journal. On her birthday, we had our dinner alone at a small camp stove. Birthdays felt like they were meant to be celebrated with just the family. I managed to find a bag of marshmallows on one of the scouting trips and hid them as a special treat. She seemed genuinely excited. I wished it could have been more, or better, but roasting marshmallows on a roof was the best we could do.

Garett had no interest in celebrating but I made him push through the motions. Emma had asked to help, and once I told him it was important to her, he let it go. We had adopted Emma into our small group after her father died. Mick felt we owed her father after what happened, but there was never really any other option. Garett was head over heels in love with her and I didn't have it in me to leave her alone to fend for herself. She didn't have the wits to make it on her own, and she was pretty enough to be scooped up by someone with bad intentions. Her naivety made her a target, and I've seen too much innocence destroyed in this new world.

"There were less zombies last night than we are used to seeing in this area."

"That's good to know. Maybe we can convince whoever is in charge today to let us get further than a mile before we stop for a look see."

"Wouldn't that be nice," he replied flatly. "Emma's with me, and you and Mick got Zoe today."

"Fine by me, I am sure you want some alone time after being lookout all night. Just promise you'll be careful."

He huffed at me in that way only teenagers can, making me feel like I was two inches tall for even insinuating that he was unable to care for the two of them. It wasn't that I felt he was incapable because god knows there are times he has saved me from my own stupidity. It was concern out of caring. I love those three kids, and I just need to know they're going to be alright.

Morning pack-ups usually went like clockwork. Even with our newest members, we moved like a machine. There was no chatter, no need for it. Everyone had a job, and since the routine was a daily occurrence, they knew how to do it without instruction. It took less than an hour to get the entire camp packed, cars and trucks loaded, and safety checks done. Wayne was in the lead, which always made me feel a perk in my step.

Mick took the wheel and Zoe climbed in the back of the Durango we had recently picked up. It was a real gas hog but it could get around pretty good without being too big. Plus, in a pinch, all five of us could cram into it. After grumbling from the back seat for a minute or two, Zoe's breathing turned soft and steady as she drifted off for her morning nap. She was a sound sleeper so I knew that Mick and I could discuss whatever we wanted without much chance of her overhearing us.

Wayne started the caravan off slow and steady. Mick and I were hoping he'd push us along until dinner. The roads in the area had been cleared by others making their way through. They weren't cleared completely but most of the debris had been pushed to the sides to clear a path, leaving small areas that were still barely passable only every few miles or so. By noon I was almost giddy. We had passed four towns that looked promising and Wayne just barreled along without stopping.

"He keeps this up, and I say we stay."

"I was just thinking the same thing, but how likely is it that we can manage to convince the others that this is the way we need to be moving every day?" Mick grumbled, obviously not caught up with the same optimism I felt.

Zoe was still out. Teenagers are weird that way. They require a ridiculous amount of sleep. They also have their days and nights reversed. Makes them good for night watch. I really don't mind them sleeping as long as we are in a safe place. Hell, I wish I could close my eyes and dream this existence away most days. Wayne pulled us into a rest stop. Gas run and bathroom break. I was just happy he found a place we could do that quickly.

Mick hopped out and ran up to the lead car as I slid over to the driver's seat. I rolled the window down and craned my head out, hoping to hear what was being discussed. I was a few car lengths too far to hear the conversation, but I could tell from the flailing arms on some of the preppers that not everyone was as jazzed as I was about our progress. Mick looked frustrated but was smart enough to let Wayne handle them. Damn, I hated when that man is right. There was no way we could convince the others to move any faster than a snail's pace.

Garett, on the other hand, looked like he was going to take a swing at one of the men. I whistled sharply to get his and Mick's attention, hoping to diffuse the situation. Mick looked in my direction but not Garett. I pointed frantically but before Mick could decipher my gestures, Garett cocked his arm back and his fist connected with the face of one of the other drivers. Mick lunged for Garett as he dove on top of the man, slamming fist after fist in the guy's face.

I couldn't see who Garett had on the ground before Mick finally got a grip on him and ripped the stubborn teenager off. Garett was fighting every step but Mick dragged him back to our truck and threw him in the back seat. He landed right on Zoe.

"Ow! What the hell!" Garett yelped. "You know damn well that jackass deserved it!"

"Doesn't matter Garett! Jesus!" Mick fumed for a bit, slowly calming himself as he paced back and forth next to the car. "Damn it, Garett! You put us in such a shitty position here."

Emma came running to Garett's side, which was also against the rules. Whenever we made a quick stop, we needed to leave drivers in each car in case we needed to take off quickly. Otherwise your driverless vehicle would be blocking the exit of all the other cars. This was due to our ever-expanding group. There had once been a time when the middle cars could still position themselves with an out. Emma didn't care for the rules much since her dad died, though. She said that rules didn't save him, so what was the point.

"Garett! Your face!" She cradled his chin in her small hands as concern washed over her face.

"It's nothing, Em. I promise. I'm fine."

"You're fine! Well whoop-de-fuckin-do, Garett! You sit here and wait while I go back and sort this shit out." Mick huffed as he stormed off towards the group.

I figured it was best to not form an opinion until I had an idea of what was going on, so in my calmest voice, I asked Garett what had happened. Amazingly, it worked and I received an answer without attitude or defensiveness.

"He threatened Em. He's been pushing it with me for a few weeks now. Even went so far as to come find me on watch one night and try to trade me supplies in exchange for a night or two with her. This time he said it would be a shame if something happened and I couldn't watch out for her. An accident or something. He promised he would 'Take care of her for me'. That was when I had enough. He was threatening us both in front of everybody, and everyone is too P.C. to do anything about it. I'm tired of keeping my cool for a group that doesn't have my back."

I took a minute to let all that sink in. He was right. I knew Mick knew it too, but he needed to calm the situation down. "Mick and I have been considering leaving the group for a while now. I wish you would have told me what was happening earlier, but it is what it is. We can't change what just went down, so now we move forward. We can't just take off, but I do agree with you, Garett. This isn't working anymore."

"What about Em?"

"I can't believe you feel like you have to ask. She's family. She comes with us. Right now, we're lucky that you're only two cars back. When there's a chance to change that, you take it. I want you two right behind me. Understand?" I paused long enough to catch a nod from him. "Now, go back and sit in your car. Get a drink, eat something. Be ready to go. You talk to no one. Lock your doors and stay in line until we take off. Be smart, Garett. If you want to take care of Em, you have to think ten steps ahead of where we are right now. You didn't do that when you cold cocked that jerk. I'm not mad about it. But you need to just go and do what I say this time, no back talk."

They walked off hand in hand and I smiled. I was happy for them. Life may have sucked compared to how it used to be, but at least they had each other, which was so important. My brother had raised his boy the right way. Just thinking of him and my sister in law broke my heart all over again. They should be the ones here with their kids. I bet all three would still be alive. Instead they got me. I somehow inherited a herd of orphans who don't know the truth. I'm not full of any wisdom, at least no more than they have. I'm just faking it.

5

Daniel

I was about done with these assholes. I couldn't help but think of them as anything but lately. And I was tired of their whining, sand bagging asses. A trip that should have taken weeks was now looking more like months and the closer we got to the coordinates on the flyer, the slower we moved. Every snapping twig, every flutter of wings in the woods, every shadow held an uncountable horde of the undead, and they scattered. Even though our group had swelled to nearly seventy men, women and children, there weren't more than five I trusted with the guns they carried. But I made a promise to the Rev, and I owed it to him to keep that promise.

After chasing me down on that roadside, he was the only one that actually forgave me for what happened between the two of us. Every other one of these assholes still harbored some resentment or another, some of them still blamed me for what happened back at Sanctuary. You know, I never heard anybody call it that while we were there, but Francine started it one night and it was like we had been calling it that all along. I didn't even really blame them for hating me. They needed a scapegoat. They needed somebody to crucify, but they also needed somebody to tell them when to shit and which direction to wipe. The Rev and I were okay, but I was getting tired of babysitting.

At the pace we were moving it would be another month before we made to this mythical compound. I had to figure it would be in ruins by the time we got there. The closer we got to anywhere that used to be populated, the worse it got. And we had skirt way wide of Philly when it came time to cross into New Jersey. No telling how much time we lost there, but no way was I going into a city that size, with or without this group in tow.

We picked up stragglers along the way. The Rev said we had a duty to and no matter how much I argued about spreading our dwindling rations even further for people that couldn't carry their own weight, he would just look at me and say, "As you have done to the least of my children, so you have done unto me." I guess quoting the Bible at me was his way of winning an argument. It worked though, I gotta give him that. He'd start in with Job, or Matthew, or 5th Corinthians or whatever, and I would throw up my hands and walk away. That shit was his crutch, not mine. Didn't matter that for every wandering soul we added to the group, we lost two or three the next day. They were tired, starving... Hell, I was tired and starving, some of them just didn't have what it takes to survive the way things are now.

See, most of these people used to live in a world where the next meal was as close as the fridge and only as far away as a drive to the store. You could lock your front door and feel safe enough to sleep through the night. Ten thousand steps a day on your pedometer was some kind of fucking accomplishment.

And the real scary shit went down in some other neighborhood, in some other country. All that was gone now, and just wanting to survive wasn't going to cut it. The softest ones went first, and they went fast. I've seen people die in a lot of different ways, but watching someone starve to death, or walk themselves to death is even more fucked up than watching them get torn apart by moaners. And we saw way more of them than we did living people.

We did run into one "gang" that tried to block our way. They looked like they might have been tough at one point, but now they were in even worse shape than us. I think they were trying to make us believe that there were more of them behind the burned out cars they had stacked in the road, and that there were reinforcements in the buildings lining the street, but I could tell right away their leader was bluffing. He knew we had the numbers. He had no way of knowing that most of the people on our side of the rubble wouldn't have been able to hit a target at half that distance with the weapons they were carrying. He also knew, probably because I told him from around the sight of my '16, that I would make sure that no matter what went down, if they tried to stop us, he would be the first one to get his fucking head blown off. After a tense few minutes, they moved aside and let us pass. I kept my weapon on him until we were almost completely out of sight. I wish we faired that well when we ran into the fucking moaners. You can't out-bluff them. You can either fight or run, and we were too tired to do either.

The only reason any of us were left at this point was that we didn't come across more than three or four bigger groups of them. That, and one giant swarm.

We had just crossed the Delaware Memorial bridge into the

southern part of New Jersey. We were still on the overpass and that's probably what saved our lives. Below us in the streets were hundreds, if not thousands, of those fucking things shuffling around aimlessly. A couple of the Townies started freaking out. I hushed everyone up pretty quick by pointing out that they had no idea we were up there and if we wanted to stay alive, it was probably a good idea to keep it that way. I had to hope they would thin out by the time we got to an off-ramp, it had taken over an hour to navigate the bridge with the mass of wrecked and abandoned vehicles blocking the road.

We continued along the interstate for another two miles, all the while watching the unending mass of undead below. It was un-fucking-real to see that many zombies in one place, you couldn't see the end of them. They just moved around slump-shouldered and silent. The first off ramp we came to was so choked with cars that the moaners couldn't have gotten to us even if they knew we were there. An hour later we came to a full interchange. One of the four ramps was completely destroyed, like somebody set a bomb off underneath it. Given the wreckage of charred vehicles and blackened skeletons, that's exactly what may have happened.

According to the map, and the road signs, we had moved onto the Turnpike. We were still moving roughly east and as long as all we ran into up here was the occasional rotting, bloated meatbag stuck inside a car (admittedly fucking disgusting, but mostly harmless), I didn't see any rush to get down to ground level and try to contend with what looked like a damn meat grinder on legs. Later on, I would regret the fuck out of that decision, but fuck it, we had places to be.

6

Vincent

The air in Loveladies always seemed better somehow. Standing on the back porch of the oversized oceanfront mansion we had moved into, I took a deep calming breath. It's been two months since I lost her. I can't seem to get a straight answer from anyone on this island when it comes to Jessica. She was here when I marched down to the line to single handedly bring order back to our side of the island. But when I went to share my victory with her, I arrived to discover an empty room. The guards all pointed fingers at whose turn it was to keep watch, so I slaughtered them all.

There were always more people in line willing to be the extra muscle that I needed, but Jessica was different. She was special. I spent two months trying to replace her and have been met with nothing but failure. I refuse to let this setback hold me back from fulfilling the future that I am destined to achieve. Even though, I found someone capable of continuing my memoir in her place, he isn't a writer of Jessica's caliber. Not many authors are though. How many internationally renowned authors existed before the apocalypse?

Finding a substitute for her other purpose has been much more challenging. I gave up on waiting for a woman to get infected and show immunity naturally. The men were ordered to bring me a new candidate each day, two as of late. Each was exposed, and each died. The plebs are getting restless, but they are blind to the true need of these sacrifices. My higher purpose is more important than the lives of a few women who would have been dead months earlier without my generous invitation into our kingdom.

I have decided to move on to my next plan. It may not be possible to find another woman like Jessica. I need to move forward with passing my genes into the next generation if we are to survive as a race. Another set of my men are looking for the best candidates to carry children for me. They will be impregnated, then the children will be tested for immunity after their birth. A mansion of this size can comfortably hold a dozen women, guards, and all our citizens with medical backgrounds. Every king deserves his castle, and I have happily conquered mine.

Earl is constantly bitching about the morale in the camp. He seems to think that it would be in our best interest to "throw them a bone every once in a while" as he puts it. I tried to explain to him that I can't be bothered with the little things, but he still kept complaining. That was when I put him in charge of doling out some comforts to the people within our walls. Not too many though, I wasn't positive they had earned the right to be too comfortable. You would think that just the act of keeping them alive would be enough, but it wasn't, and deep down that offended me.

It seemed that no matter how much you gave them, they always wanted more. They cried for houses. So, I gave them to them, but the houses were too small. So, I moved them to bigger ones. Then, they complained that the furniture inside wasn't nice enough, or the clothes didn't fit. They wanted new things, nice things. I told Earl to grant their wishes. "Do whatever they want, just keep them happy," I said.

I was a kind ruler. But my patience wore thin. The demands got more ridiculous by the day. The final straw was when Earl came to me asking that we send a search party out to find gluten-free food. That was when I saw that I had allowed my subjects to cross a line that may become my undoing. They were no longer afraid of me, or grateful to be alive. They were reverting back to the same spoiled lumps that they were before the outbreak occurred. It was time to teach them a lesson.

When darkness fell, and they fell asleep with full bellies in their fluffy beds drunk off of wine they had demanded so rudely, I asked my men to move the fence five blocks back. Once the line was moved, they opened the gates and knocked away the walls that separated half of them from the army of undead that roamed the other side of the island. Earl begged for leniency, but I grew tired of his advice on this subject. If it wasn't for his firsthand knowledge of my greatness, I am sure I would have thrown him on the other side of the fence with the others. I have no use for those that question my orders.

As I lay my head down as day broke, on what surely was a hundred-dollar pillow, I was serenaded by the screams of those sacrificed to prove my point. Rest came fast and easy, and as usual the world disappeared as I closed my eyes. The funny thing was that no one ever brought a request in front of me again. Turns out, as usual, I was completely right in how to handle those in my care.

7

Jeremy

For the first time in months, I was able to race down a road. I settled into a calm as the needle pushed towards 80 mph. Trees blurred past and my mind cleared. It was like a glimpse of my life before, speeding down the road to nowhere with nothing but my thoughts. I had finally had it with the dimwits that I had been traveling with for the last few weeks. I packed up and took off in the middle of the night. Doubling back to the old mustang that I had seen a few miles back, I hit the somewhat open road.

The final straw was when Crystal made a pass at me in front of Big Ben that was obvious enough that even a blind man could see what she was aiming at. In the beginning, I thought she had just taken a shine to me, but what was really happening was she was bored. When the walking got long and monotonous, she would poke the bear to see if she could get a reaction out of him. She was just using me as part of some tired old game that women had been playing for years.

I probably should have been upset that she had no interest in me, but my ego didn't need to be fed by the attentions of some high maintenance apocalypse queen. It is a sad state of affairs when you aren't worth fighting over even if you are the last woman alive. So, I looked for a way out of that precarious situation. If I wasn't trying to escape, I may have pointed out the mustang as we hiked past it. Crystal was too busy telling one of her glory day stories about her days on the stage to notice the car sitting like a sore thumb in the parking lot we crossed through. She kept insisting she was a singer, but I still held a belief that singing was code for stripping. It was a bit strange that we never heard her sing for us if she was really a singer. I never pressed the issue though, it seemed like it may earn me a right hook from Ben.

My uneasiness grew as we walked further away from the car. I needed to find that goldilocks zone when it came to the car, not too far for me to walk, and not too close for them to hear the engine roar to life. We were covering too much ground, so I faked a fall over a log. That resulted in us having to take an hour break just to let me rest my newly injured ankle. When I felt enough time had been burned in one place, I got ready for the best acting I had ever preformed in my life. My limp was one for the books, and each moan made my companions wince at the sound of my pain.

We made it another half mile to a parking lot of a shopping center. Sad to say, but I was pretty sure this one was dead long before the rise of zombies. The anchor stores were empty and all that had made it to the end of civilization was a pizzeria named Eli's, a puppy mill pet store, and one of those "We buy gold" shops. Crystal, self-centered as always, convinced Ben to take her on a shopping trip to find something shiny to hang around her neck. She explained that, once they found a big enough group of people, gold would be worth something again.

I knew it was bullshit. She knew it was bullshit. Ben, on the other hand, wouldn't know bullshit if it smacked him in the face, and was going to end up with a backpack filled with useless trinkets that he would have to lug around like some kind of end-of-the-world pack mule. That gave me the opportunity to start setting up camp. There were a few busted up cars that weren't road worthy but would give us enough protection from the monsters wandering around to get a good night's sleep. It was a small blessing that people didn't have enough time to lock their doors as they abandoned their vehicles. They may have been too distracted running away from zombies, or they figured that it was already broken so who cares?

I wasn't planning on sticking around, but that didn't mean I didn't want to make sure they were safe on my way out. By the time Crystal had Ben lugging a suitcase that looked like it weighed a ton back to the spot where I was resting with my fake busted leg up, I already had dinner roasting on the fire.

"Aren't they beautiful?" she purred as she leaned in to show me two teardrop diamonds that hung from her ears.

"Gorgeous," I said, showing just enough interest to appease her, but not enough to tick of her body guard. "Did you two clear the place out?"

"I couldn't make up my mind and Ben said he would be willing to carry all of it. We are going to live like royalty once we make our way back to people. Hopefully by then, I will know which ones I can part with. I mean they all look so nice on me." She pouted as she dished herself a plate and sat staring at us. "Well, aren't you hungry?"

"Yeah, but my leg is acting up. Do you think we could just call it a night after dinner? I want to give it some time resting to see if it feels better." I asked hoping she would pick up the hint and make a plate for myself and Ben.

It was so frustrating watching him follow her like a puppy dog. She just wasn't good people. Someone who cared for others would feed the injured first. I knew I was faking it, but she didn't. And Ben was willing to carry a few hundred pounds of gold around to make her happy, and she couldn't even toss some chili on a plate for him. There definitely wasn't going to be a knock down drag em' out fight for that woman. Ben could have her.

He grunted at me as he slopped two giant spoonfuls of the slop onto two plates and handed one to me as he sat down. He was good people. Not too bright, but he deserved so much better than the two of us. He wasn't lying to get an opening to take off, and he wasn't a self-centered floozy, but that is who he ended up with. It almost made me feel bad enough to stay. Almost.

After dinner, I crawled into the cab of the smallest car I could find. I wanted to make sure it was going to be only me in it as we tucked in for the night. I packed up everything that I felt entitled to and did my best at faking sleep. Crystal made her way over to my car and jiggled the handle only to be met with a locked door. Not even worth a roll in the hay on the way out. If my friends could only see me now. They would be proud of me for having some standards. That was something I was lacking back in the days when only the living were up and walking around.

My leg felt a bit weird from all the limping I had done over the last few hours, but it wore off pretty quick once I was able to move with a little less tiptoe. By the time I made it back to the Mustang, I was moving at a full run. The next part was a bit trickier but being out on the road and hanging out with who would have been the wrong crowd before, taught me how to get a car moving without the keys. The delinquents were more useful than the goody two-shoes these days.

I drove through a few towns before I got out of the wreckage and into the clear. This part of South Jersey was filled with long stretches of narrow roads that slashed through miles of farmland. People forget that it's called the Garden State. All they seem to remember is the crap they saw on cable TV. Most of this state is green in one way or another, and not covered in oil refineries or guidos. Hell, even the northern part of the state will be taken back by nature soon enough.

The sun peeked over the horizon, and I knew it was probably a good time to stop. No reason to try driving head on into a blind spot. It was too wide open for me to just pull over and fall asleep. The dead really aren't an issue if you are locked away sleeping in a giant steel machine. It was the living that might wander up and see this sweet ass ride and put a bullet in my head for it. So, I started searching the horizon for a safe place to pull in before I drifted off into nothingness.

After an hour or so of frustration, I was rewarded with Small Town USA. Nothing more than an old, long abandoned gas pump and a few of busted up farm houses. That gas pump was dry long before the apocalypse. The signs above it read 64 cents a gallon and I don't think it ever ran on electric. This would be the perfect place to pull in and get some shut eye. There wasn't anything worth sticking around for, so I was almost positive it was empty.

I clicked the tape deck off and pulled in as quietly as you can in a Mustang running on fumes. I turned the keys but didn't pull them out. If there was trouble, there was no way I was wasting time trying to find them and get the engine turned over.

In movies, those moments make for the best, most suspenseful moments, but in real life those extra seconds are life and death. Damn, I was tired. I didn't realize it until I stopped.

Well, there go any plans I had for making myself some food. My eyes, heavy with exhaustion, fought my every attempt to keep them open. My stomach growled, and hunger pains shot through my gut, but I just couldn't catch that second wind. Just a few minutes rest, I lied to myself. I allowed myself to drift off and thanked God the night wasn't filled with the snores of Big Ben. With my last moment awake my head fell to the side, and I could swear I saw a sliver of light from the attic window of one of the old farmhouses. Too late now, I would have to check on it in a bit later in the morning.

8

Ian

"Listen to me very carefully, and please let me finish before you freak out." I leaned close to Ken and locked eyes to show him that, despite being extremely drunk on stolen scotch, I was in fact completely serious. While he was just as hammered as I was he nodded an affirmative and leaned back in his lawn chair.

"I need you to help me figure something out. Something big. I've been turning it over and over in my head trying to figure out what the hell it means, but I'm no good with this kind of shit." I paused for a minute trying to pick the right words out of the slurry running through my mind. "You know I was a soldier, and that I came here from Virginia. What I never told anybody was what I was doing there." I filled Ken in on the details of Bentonville, and the short series of events leading up to the line I knew would knock him on his ass. "It was my sergeant. I thought he needed my help, but as I reached out to grab him and drag him out from under the vehicle, he sank his teeth into my wrist up to the gums."

The color drained from Ken's face, but he sat and listened to the rest of my tale like he promised he would. I told him about the hospital and the testing and finally getting out after killing that fucking doctor. Then I told him about William's scar and the story he told me about his parents.

Ken bolted out of his chair. I thought he was going to take off toward the nearest guard, but he leapt at me grabbed my shoulders and, completely sober now, shouted, "Do you have any idea what this means!? Please tell me you aren't fucking with me. This means we could develop some kind of vaccine, or even a cure! We have to get Mike, we have to get everyone!"

It was then that he took off toward the command center, assumedly to wake up the entire leadership staff and anybody else within earshot. I got up and followed, figuring there'd be some questions I would have to answer.

By the time I made it to the conference room, set up in one of the airport's old managers' offices, Ken had already rounded up half a dozen of those that served as command. They sat around the table, some obviously still trying to shake the sleep from their brains.

"What the hell so important Ken?" John, the electrical engineer, spoke up first, but as soon as he had a murmur of agreement rumbled through the others at the table.

"We need to wait for Mike. Trust me, this is huge."

John wafted his hand theatrically in front of his face. "Jesus, Ken, how drunk are you?"

"Never mind all that, John. Ian has some information that you all need to hear."

All eyes turned to me. I shrugged and sat down, "Ken's right. Once everyone is here I'll drop my bomb on you. Better to only have to tell it once."

After a few minutes, Mike came through the door and as

matter-of-factly as always, took his seat at the table. "Anybody want to tell me what the fuck this is all about, please?"

"We were wondering that ourselves, Mike," came the reply from the others. John added, "Apparently, Ian has some big news that required us all to be dragged out of bed."

Mike leveled his gaze at me and raised his eyebrows.

I relayed the details of my story, then William's, the same way I told Ken an hour before. I got pretty much the reaction I expected too. A lot of shaking heads, dropped jaws, and Mike sitting there with his brow furrowed, mulling the whole thing over. They fired questions at me one after another as I did my best to keep up. No, I had no idea if there were others at the hospital with my immunity. No, I had no idea how common it might be. No, I had no idea why I was immune to whatever the hell was causing this. Everybody wanted to see the scar I had worked so hard to hide since arriving few a few months ago.

Finally, Mike spoke up. "You were in this hospital for what, two, maybe three months? From what it sounds like, they were running tests on you the whole time while the rest of the country went to shit. They had to have made some kind of progress in figuring this out. Maybe they were even close to a cure. Maybe there is some way we can pick up where they left off." He turned to Ken. "This is what you did right? Researching diseases and finding ways to fight them?"

Ken replied, "It's a little more complicated than that, but basically, yes, I was an epidemiologist. But if you're suggesting that I would somehow be able to figure out what an entire building full of scientists couldn't… With no equipment and no staff… It would be impossible."

"What if we can get you the equipment?" asked one of the

committee members, "There are several agricultural research facilities around here. They might have what you need."

Ken's face twisted in thought. "There's... There's no way. I mean, we're talking about the C.D. fucking C. here. There's no way I can even replicate their conditions, let alone their research capabilities, their resources..." He trailed off shaking his head. Ken got up from the table and began pacing along the wall. "We're talking about one chance in a trillion that I could even make progress on the research they had done, if I even had access to it!"

I stood slowly, leaned over the table and rested my weight on my knuckles. "I'll go back and get it."

"Get what?!" Ken exclaimed.

"Their research. There have to be files, laptops, samples, something you can use. I'll go get it. I'll take my Humvee and my weapon and..."

"And WHAT?!" Ken repeated. "You haven't got a fucking clue what I need! No offense. You're a hell of a soldier, but you're no scientist. You would know the first place to look or what kind of files to grab."

"Then come with me." I said. "I'll get you inside and you can snag whatever you think you'll need. I know it's a longshot. Hell, you're probably right and it's a pointless effort, but these people need something to hope for, don't they? How long before morale completely craps out in this place? How long before people decide to just give up? Not long if there's no hope for any kind of future. The people here are waiting for a cavalry that's never fucking coming, but only the people in this room know that. How long before these people figure that out?! I'm going. Come with me, stay here, I don't care, but I'm not just going to sit here and wait for a swarm of those fucking things to overrun the fence, or to die of some fucking papercut with my thumb in my ass. I don't know why I waited so long to tell any of you about getting bitten. I had my reasons, but I waited too long. Maybe we can do something about what's going on out there, and I am not going to give up what may be the one chance I have to make a difference." I fell back in my chair, out of breath.

Mike spoke up, "Ian, what makes you think I'm going to just let you take valuable resources away from our effort here to run off on some wild goose chase to Virginia?" My jaw dropped, then a smirk slowly spread across his normally inexpressive face. "It's risky as hell, Ian. I have no real love for the idea of letting you grab one of the few vehicles we have left and take my best soldier on a 300-mile road trip. But I also think you're right. We need to do something, anything we can to try and keep the human race going. If the last 8 months are any indication, we don't have much time before this war is over."

There were mixed reactions from around the table, but nobody voiced any real strong dissent. Ken looked exasperated. Funny, this meeting was his idea. What the hell did he expect? For everybody to just say 'Okay, there's some random percentage of the population that's immune for some reason or another. Let's just leave it at that and go on farming next to the landing strip.'

"Maybe they figured out what caused this mess…" Ken said, taking off his glasses and running the fingers of his other hand through his shaggy, graying hair. "That's step one. The only way to fight it is to know what the hell it is. From the conference I was at that landed me here, I can tell you that nobody in the civilian world had a clue, but maybe the government did. I'm going to have to go with you. It's the only way to know for sure that some vital piece of data doesn't get left behind. Mike, I'm going to make a list of equipment. Maybe we can send scouts to go find it."

Mike nodded. "How many men do you think you'll need Ian?"

I shrugged again, "I'd have to plan it out. I don't want to take an entire regiment with me. Smaller groups move faster, but I would need to pick the right guys."

"William?"

I thought about what almost happened the last time I took William through Virginia and shook my head. "No, I think he'd be better off here with you. He likes you, he'll follow your orders."

Mike nodded again in understanding. "Take the night. Plan your route, figure out the logistics and report to me in the morning with your wish list. We'll figure it out then." He rose to his feet. "Gentlemen, if there is nothing else, I would really like to get some sleep before my fire guard shift." With that, he did a smart about-face and left.

Ken had the final word, "I need another drink."

9

Max and Rocky

Rocky wasn't growling. That was new. Most of the time, when someone new got too close to us, he'd let out a low, deep growl. That was my sign that we needed to head out somewhere new. We had been on our own for at least a month now. I lost track of counting the nights around day 5. I just didn't care. They were gone, and all their nonsense with them. Sometimes I wonder how they are doing, but most of the time, I don't.

I peeked out the attic window to see what the noise was and saw a car pull up slowly under the roof at the gas station. They shut the car off but didn't get out. I waited forever to see if they were going to start looking for stuff. I knew even if they did that all the good stuff was gone and I hoped that would get them to leave. Instead I sat there watching like an idiot for a really long time before I figured out that whoever was in that car had gone to sleep as soon as they pulled in. Sheesh. What a waste. I could have been asleep the whole time, too.

I looked over at Rocky and started scratching his big fluffy ears. "Man, that was dumb. I should have known right away. You knew."

He pushed his head into my lap and licked my fingers. I know my Dad would be proud of the two of us. He told me I had to grow up too quick, and I hoped I was doing right by him. But I know he would be happy that me and Rocky were still sticking it out together, keeping each other safe. I gave him a few more scratches, then curled up in my sleeping bag. "Lights out again, boy," I mumbled as I fell back asleep.

Rocky wasn't growling so I knew he thought it was safe for me to rest for a bit more. Rocky always had my back. If he felt it was time to move, he would tell me. Once I felt him lay down across my feet, I was out. I don't know when Rocky really sleeps. Even at night he is watching out for me. I guess dogs can live on no sleep. I'm not a vet, how would I know?

Morning always comes too fast. Even before the zombies, I liked to lay in bed way too late. On a farm, you have to be out of bed when it is still dark if you want to get your chores done before you head off to school. I was always jealous of my friends who lived in small houses in town. They could get up and watch a cartoon or two while they ate some cereal on their couch. Not me, I was out there mucking the barn or some other activity that wasn't cartoons.

Now, more often than not. I wake up early because most adults don't. They stay awake too long at night, afraid the monsters lurking in the dark will find them. The problem with those kinds of thoughts is that the monsters are around all the time. The dark only makes them look scarier, but they can get you in the sunshine, too. So, I try to get up early, and Rocky and I sneak out of our hiding place and get on the road again. We were running a bit behind this time, but not by too much.

I packed up all our gear as quickly as I could and started munching on a few of the apples I had found yesterday in an old orchard. They were perfectly ripe. I never knew that New Jersey had farms like the one where I grew up. I was glad they did, though. It made it easier to find food for right now. The fall harvest season was going to come and go without anyone picking those delicious apples off the trees. It was a shame, but I couldn't sit around for apples.

Rocky's ears perked up just as I reached for the attic door. On the other side was a scraggly looking man who seemed just as surprised to see me as I was to see him. I have no idea why it took Rocky that long to hear someone coming up the stairs. He definitely wasn't acting like himself. Normally, he would be biting at my backside to make me move faster if he thought there was someone getting close. I think Rocky was sick of other people, too. They were nothing but trouble.

"Jesus, kid. Scared the shit out of me. What are you doing alone up here? The rest of your group out looking for supplies or something?"

I stared at the man for a minute trying to size him up. He didn't seem like a threat, but you could never be too sure. It's best not to let your guard down too much around here. Rocky was wagging his tail like he had found a long-lost friend. Maybe this guy wasn't going to be a problem.

"Where's your group?" I asked, figuring I would change the subject. I didn't want him to know I was alone, but I wasn't big on lying either.

"I ditched them a while back. They were getting on my nerves. I try not to stay with anyone too long, anyway. I'm heading somewhere and I want to get there as fast as I can. Groups just slow you down."

"Yeah," I agreed, nodding my head as I made my way past the stranger. I wanted to get down the stairs and out the door in case I needed to bolt. He didn't try to block my way, so that was another plus on his side.

"You going somewhere, kid?" He asked in a way that sounded more like it was out of curiosity than accusation.

"Yeah, some fort. Well, maybe. I haven't decided yet."

"You haven't decided?" I could see the wheels turning. Damn, it. I gave away that it was just me and Rocky. No grown up would let a kid be in charge. "This fort?" He held out the flyer.

"Yeah. I had a group." I figured there was no point in hiding it now. "They got kind of crazy, though, so I took off. Rocky and me were on our own before we found them anyway."

"Well, nice to meet you Rocky. My name's Jeremy," he said, holding his hand out for Rocky to sniff before reaching down and scratching Rocky like a madman. "It's been a while since I've seen a dog. Bet he likes belly rubs. Do you like belly rubs?" He asked before rolling onto the grass with Rocky.

They rolled around in the dirt and grass for a good five minutes before either one acknowledged that I existed. Rocky ran off to grab a stick and must have remembered that I was standing there waiting for him. He ran over and put the slobbery stick in my hand. I scanned the field and there didn't seem to be any moaners, but I decided the road was a better place since I could see the ground, too.

Rocky took off like a shot after the stick. This was the first time in a long time I got to see him play. Come to think of it, I couldn't remember the last time we played fetch. I tried not to let my guard down, but after a few tosses, I was so busy watching Rocky fly back and forth down the street that I had stopped paying attention to the world around me. That was when Jeremy screamed.

"Damn it! Grab your stuff, kid, we have to go!" He yelled as he struggled away from a moaner who had grabbed him by the shirt. He spun around two or three times as fast as he could and slipped out of the ratty flannel he was wearing. The moaner dropped to the ground but he was being followed closely by two more undead buddies, so I decided the best bet was to follow this man until we were out of trouble. I scooped up my sack and ran after him into the garage.

He whistled loudly for Rocky, who abandoned his stick and bolted into the garage ahead of us. That dog was always a step or two ahead. Climbing into the old junker, I had a brief second of regret. I really had no reason to link myself up with another person. Rocky and I were doing just fine without anyone else. The engine suddenly revved so loud that there was no changing my mind right now. Every moaner in a mile radius would be heading our way to see what all the commotion was about.

"Sorry, kid. I should have been watching. I got too wrapped up in your dog. What's your name, anyway? I never asked," he said casually as he plowed over the three corpses trying to stop us from leaving.

"Max. Where are we headed?"

"The place on the paper. I can drop you off whenever you want, but for now let's just hang together until we're out of Crazytown."

"Okay for right now, but I still don't know if I want to go there." I started to think about the Rev and Daniel. If I went to the place they were heading to I would have to deal with them and all their bullshit.

"Fine by me, kid. You hungry? I got some cans in the backseat. Crack open a few, can opener is with them. I think I have dog food, too. It may be gross but it is food. You can give that to Rocky. I am sure he needs to eat after all that running. I have water, too."

"Thanks, Jeremy," I said as I flipped over into the backseat. I pulled my bag over and reached inside. The metal dog bowl was gross but it still held stuff. I filled it with water and then food. Once Rocky had his fill, he rolled away from me and fell sound asleep for the first time since we were with Daniel. I crawled back to the front, trying not to wake him. He deserved the rest.

"Peaches and spaghetti circles okay?"

"No name brand left? Ah, well. Store brand will have to do," Jeremy laughed to himself at a joke that I didn't entirely get.

We spent the next hour or so listening to music I had never heard before on the car radio. Jeremy seemed to forget that I was even around anymore. Each song was "my jam." I laid back and listened to him sing along as I watched the grass and trees roll by. Eventually, we puttered out of gas.

"I filled up with what I could find laying around in that garage before I came up and found you. It got us further than I thought it would," he said while scanning the area. "There were a few houses a mile or so back. You stay here and guard the car. I'm going to walk back and see if I can get us some fuel or a better ride. This one guzzles gas."

He didn't wait for me to agree. He just popped the trunk, pulled out a gas can, and headed out. Rocky was already awake and on watch again. I guess he felt like his time off was over. I scratched his ears and poured him some more water. Can't have him watching for moaners with a dry mouth.

"You think we should stay?" I asked as I scratched in between his ears, hoping once again that God would grant Rocky the ability to talk. "Fine. I'll make the call this time, but you have dibs on the next big decision."

Rocky stared in my eyes, and I could swear he nodded. So, there it was, we were going to stay. At least for now. If this guy does a turn and starts acting nutty we are out of here. Hopefully I had some time to figure out if I wanted to head to the place on the paper. The open road was calling, but that place might have a home cooked meal. So many choices.

10

Reverend Mathis

I cannot decide which is worse, the physical toll this journey has taken on my body, or the spiritual torment I must endure daily. This relentless uncertainty and confusion has swept over me. Is my faith being tested, or have I strayed so far from the Lord's path that He has abandoned me? After bringing Daniel back into the fold as it were, many of the remaining townies voiced their dissent. I understand the ill will they bore toward him as many of them blamed him for what had happened at Sanctuary. I blamed him myself for a while. As days turned into weeks, my anger faded and I began to see my own culpability in what had occurred. Nevertheless, there were those in what remained of our group that still harbored resentment.

That day on the road when Daniel agreed to come with us to the location on the flyer, I naively believed that simply because I told them to, the townies would accept him back, but after the collapse of Sanctuary and the savage beating I received at his hands, they never looked at him the same way again. Even now as we close the remaining distance to our destination, I know there are several that still blame him entirely for what happened.

As we made our way slowly east through the wreckage of civilization, I marveled at how quickly devastation had set in to the country. Everywhere we went were burned buildings, destroyed vehicles, and, of course, the dead. Sometimes they were few in numbers, sometimes they were many.

The journey should only have taken less than a month, but in our fear we moved slowly and in nowhere near an efficient path. We knew we would have to cross a bridge into New Jersey at some point and that that would mean we would have to move through a populated area. As food became harder to find and what little ammunition we had for the few guns we carried dwindled, the townies began to lose hope that we would ever make it out of Pennsylvania, let alone to the New Jersey shore. They argued nearly every night as to whether the place to which we were headed still existed, or that it was the haven we hoped for, that it was infested with zombies or cannibals or that we would simply be stripped of our supplies and sent back the way we came. I did my best to keep them strong, but words will only carry so far when stomachs are empty and feet are blistered.

The desperation of our situation became readily apparent as we crossed into New Jersey and saw a swarm of the undead even larger than the one we fled on the other side of the bridge. I did my best, as always, to keep the morale of my flock up, but the task that grew harder with each setting of the sun became impossible as my own fortitude failed at the sight of an ocean of moaning corpses.

We continued along the overpass, making slow progress through the mass of twisted and burned metal. The occasional zombie lunged at us from behind the window of a car. After a while, we were numbed to this display and saw it more as a nuisance than something to inspire fear. Several miles down the road the overpass began to slope downward as the interstate met up the ground below it. Luckily, the undead below us had begun to thin out. Still, their numbers were sufficient enough to cause many in our group to talk about going back. Daniel wouldn't hear of it. I myself entertained the thought briefly, but then had to admit that spending the rest of our lives on the overpass was no option. We would have to find a way through the throngs below if we could hope to move onward.

Daniel and I agreed to a rest stop while we planned our next move.

"There's too damned many of them to just try to run for it." Daniel said. I had to concur. While they were not as densely packed as they had been nearer the water, there were still more than we could possibly hope to fight through.

"Perhaps if we could somehow distract them," I posited.

"What I wouldn't give for a couple of frag grenades right now. That'd distract the fuckers. Blow a hole big for us to run through too."

Richard, a quiet man on most days came forward with an idea. "What about one of these cars. If we blew one of them up, that might distract them long enough for us to get away."

We mulled over the idea for a few minutes.

"I don't know Richard," I said, "With all of these cars, wouldn't it cause a chain reaction that may kill us as well?"

Richard looked a little dejected, mirroring my own growing despair at the situation.

Daniel's eyes flashed. "You're a fucking genius Rick!" We both looked at Daniel quizzically. "We turn the cars into grenades!" He shot to his feet and took off toward the nearest intact vehicle. He popped open the gas cap and stuck his nose inside. His head jerked back and his face twisted as he waved a hand in front of his own face. "Perfect!" He ran back the way we had come yelling over his shoulder as he went. "We light 'em and shove 'em over the side! If we move back a half mile or so, the ones over here will move that way to check out the noise."

It was a brilliant idea, I clapped Richard on the shoulder and got to my feet to help Daniel. We backtracked up the overpass to a point where the guardrail had been destroyed. Looking over the edge, I saw the remains of a large SUV below.

Daniel looked around. "Plenty of good candidates here. We can send them through that break in the walls." He began to rummage through his pack and removed an old t-shirt. "We need fuses. And some gas." I saw a jerry can lashed to the back a jeep that had rolled onto its side. I grabbed the can and shook it. The gas inside didn't slosh as I expected, it seemed to have thickened. I told Daniel and he was delighted.

"Jellied. Perfect for we need." He snatched the can out of my hand and began stuffing strips of t-shirt into the neck. He then turned to a sedan that was already angled toward the broken guardrail. The gas cap was locked in place so Daniel pried it off with a tire iron. He jammed several strips of gasoline-soaked rag into the neck of the gas tank and moved around to the driver's door. A long dead body slumped against the steering wheel. It showed no signs of movement. Closer inspection revealed the gunshot wound at the right temple and the large hole in the back of the skull. The small bodies in the backseat bore similar wounds. Daniel smashed out the window with the tire iron, reached in and jerked the gear shift into neutral. He also used the tire iron to knock the corpse's foot off of the brake.

"Alright everybody back up. I have no idea if this is even going to work, but I'm not taking the chance. We also don't want any of those things down there to see food up here." Those with us moved to the opposite side of the overpass as Daniel lit the fuse dangling from the gas tank and he and Richard pushed the vehicle to the edge of the road. They looked at each other once and with a final push, heaved the vehicle over. There was a loud crash followed by a commotion below as Daniel and Richard hurried over to us. We waited with bated breath for the explosion. Almost a full minute passed as we stared at each other. Just as Daniel began to slowly creep to the edge, it came. A tremendous fireball shot toward the sky and the overpass itself seemed to shake. A plume of black smoke billowed from forty feet below and the crackle of the fire mingled with the moans of the undead as they came to inspect this new stimuli. I risked a peek over the edge and saw the mangled bodies of around fifty zombies writhing on the ground around the charred remains of Daniel's makeshift bomb.

"Back up Rev, we're going again" I heard Daniel exclaim from behind me. I turned and he was trying to maneuver another sedan toward the break. Several of the men had moved to help him. Again, Daniel stuffed rags into the gas tank, set the transmission into neutral, lit the fuse and pushed the car over the edge. Again came the crash and we moved to the opposite lane and ducked behind a van. Several minutes passed this time before the explosion and the fireball. This time the bridge actually did shake and several chunks of smoking, twisted metal were thrown up onto the overpass.

Daniel sent one of the quicker men back to the main group to let them know we were okay and that the plan was working.

We decided to risk one more bomb, this time a large box van that took the five of us to move into position. Daniel told the men to begin moving back the group as soon as we pushed it over the side. He did not want to risk this section the road collapsing with us still on it.

Daniel stuffed the remaining rags into the neck of the truck's gas tank and stuck his lighter to it. He nodded to the group and we heaved the vehicle over the edge. For a moment it teetered on the lip of the drop and threatened to rock back against us. Gravity got the best of it and over it went. We moved quickly down the slope of the interstate back toward the group. When the boom came, it was significantly louder than the first two and indeed the section of bridge that we had been standing on went crashing down, presumably onto the heads of the zombies that had gathered below.

We hastened back to the main group who seemed a little more positive, even elated. The explosions had indeed thinned the ranks of the undead below us. Daniel warned against getting too excited as the noise would draw other zombies from the surrounding area. He recommended we move quickly before they arrived and the ones already here lost interest with the burning wreckage. He also cautioned against firing any weapons until we were well out of the zone, opting for the hammers, baseball bats, and lengths of pipe most of us carried.

As we descended onto the ground level we were able to dispatch the ghouls there quickly and quietly. Bolstered by the small win we had just experienced, we resumed our trek with a renewed sense of purpose. Later that evening as we set camp on the roof of a warehouse, the plume of black smoke from our afternoon's work was still just visible behind us.

After our evening meal, I went to Daniel to congratulate him and to thank him for his earlier work. He was dismissive as usual, feigning humility at the genius of his idea.

"Saw it in a movie once," was his only reply. He bent further over his can of stew and avoided eye contact.

"Still," I retorted, "we would surely have died if not for your leadership."

He bristled visibly at the word. "Don't start that shit again, Rev. I don't have the patience for this convo right now."

"But, Daniel, how can you not see the divine interventions at work here?"

"Save the sermon for the Townies, Rev. I don't need it. I'm out to save my own ass. You guys come along for the ride…" he shrugged, "call it a bonus." With that, he rose to his feet and made his way to the edge of the low, squat building.

"The men did well," I followed, not wanting to press the matter, but not wanting to let him entirely off the hook either. Again, he responded with a shrug. His lack of response infuriated me, but I could not let my emotion show. There were still many in the group that held a grudge against him for what he had done to me, even though it seemed so long ago, my face still bore some of the marks of his rage. I decided to press a little further. "Please, Daniel, consider what you bring to the group. These men and women need guidance."

He turned on me, near furious, but not raising his voice. Apparently, he thought the same as I in regard to the sensitivity of his position. "I told you to save it. I ain't a fucking leader. I'm never gonna be a leader. If I walked off now, you guys would keep going without me. Shit, you might even be better off. It just so happens we're heading in the same fucking direction. That's all." He stomped off again, the evident anger in his footfalls drawing some attention. I watched as he moved to the far end of the roof, and, unable to put any more distance between the two of us, slumped to the ground. He cast his can over the edge and it clanked on the ground drawing a moan from some ghoul wandering below.

11

William

Ian told me he was going to go back to Virginia. Ian told me I must stay here in Batsto while he goes back to Virginia with Ken. He said he will be back in a few weeks. They are going to go back to the hospital where he stayed to find some papers. I told him there are papers all over the place here, but he says they need different ones. I asked him why I cannot go with him. He said I must stay here so that Mike can continue my training. Ian said I am becoming a good soldier. I like training. I do not like doing push-ups and running, but I like marksmanship. And I like Drill. Ian tells me "Left. Face!" and "Right. Face!" and "Port. Arms!" Exactly what I am supposed to do, and I do it. Ian and Mike also say I shoot very well. Mike gave me one of his badges. He said it is an expert marksmanship badge. I got it for shooting all forty targets at my test. He said that if I want to wear it on my shirt, there is a very specific way I have to put it on. He said it is not proper to put it on a t-shirt. It must be on a jacket, and only certain kinds of jackets. It must be on the left pocket in the exact center with the top exactly one eighth of an inch below the top of the flap. Mike said he was going to set the pin for me, but Ian said that might be a bad idea. Ian told me later that it might hurt me. I did not know what he meant.

Mike has also taught me hand to hand combat. He said it would not do any good against zombies, but if someone were ever to grab me again, Mike showed me how to stomp down on the top of their foot and to use the palm of my hand to strike them in the throat and to make my hand into a claw and hit them in the eyes. Ian does not know that Mike is teaching me these things. Mike says it is not a secret and that Ian would not be mad, these are things that every soldier knows. I do not think that Ian would be mad that Mike showed me how to use my elbows to break someone's nose or to kick with the toe of my boot up under someone's kneecap. Mike wanted to show me what he called "grappling" but I did not want to do that.

Ian said I have to stay at Batsto because it will be dangerous were they are going. Ian also said that I am to listen to Mike and to follow orders. Ian said that Mike is my Commanding Officer. Mike does not speak to me as if I were stupid, which people sometimes do. I am not stupid, quite the contrary, I am very smart. I know this because Mother and Father used to point it out to people. "He's such a bright boy," they would say. I am smart enough to know that I am different, that my brain works differently than other peoples', but that does not mean I am stupid. Mike talks to me in a way that I understand, just like Ian. They do not use words they don't mean and then tell me it is a "figure of speech." I do not understand figures of speech. Why don't people just say the words that they mean, like Ian and Mike? When Ian and I were on the road coming to this place, we talked a lot. I do not normally like to talk to people. I did not really like talking to Ian at first. After we left the place where the man beat up Ian's face and Ian started to teach me how to be a soldier, I talked more because Ian asked me lots of questions. It is rude to not answer someone's questions. So Ian would ask me about baseball or television shows or astronomy and I would answer him. After a while, we just talked about anything. It was not as good as watching television, but I did not mind it too much.

The people here are nice, but they sometimes talk to me like I am stupid. They talk very slowly and over-enunciate their words. This frustrates me because it takes them even longer to tell me what they are trying to say. Ian and Mike just get straight to the point. They also use words that they do not mean, which confuses me. Then they think I am being stupid when I am just confused. One of the other soldiers patted me on the head one day. This made me very mad. The soldier laughed when I told him I was mad. I told him to stop laughing at me, that it was making me madder, but that only made him laugh harder. I stepped back into the fighting stance that Mike had shown me and raised my fists like I was trained to do. The soldier stopped laughing. He told me to put my dukes down. I did not know what 'dukes' were, and I guess my face got confused again so he started laughing again. I was so mad, but I knew that Ian would be mad at me if I 'threw the first punch'. The soldier made a face I did not understand. It was a laughing-angry-hungry-mad face. Then he dropped into the same fighting stance I was in.

"Don't try it, Retard. I'll take you apart," was what he said to me.

I have been called this name before. It always made other people madder than it made me. I remember once, I was with Mother at the grocery store. I was very young. Mother was helping me pick out some candy at the register because I had been a good boy, so I could have candy. They did not have any Mars bars. Cindy, the woman at the cash register who knew Mother and I well, was very apologetic because she knew that Mars bars were my favorite. I could not pick another candy bar and Mother was trying to help me. There were too many and I could not pick one. Mother was about to pick one for me, sometimes she had to do that if I could not choose for myself, like sometimes if we went to a new restaurant.

A man behind us in line told Mother to "Just grab a Snickers and shut that retard up!"

Everyone around us stopped what they were doing and looked over at the man. Their faces were very mad. I was not mad. I just wanted a Mars bar. Mother started yelling at the man explaining very loudly that I was not retarded. She told him that I was probably smarter than he was and that he better watch his mouth. This man laughed just like the soldier was doing now until a bigger man behind him tapped him on the shoulder. The man spun around fast, but when he saw how much bigger the other man was, he stopped laughing and looked scared.

The bigger man told the man to 'apologize to this nice, young man and his mother."

The man looked very scared. The bigger man was very big, and he had a hand on the man's shoulder. The man apologized to Mother and then to me. Mother stood there smiling at him. I do not understand why she was smiling. The man left his groceries in the cart and walked quickly out of the store. Mother thanked the bigger man and hugged him. I thought he was going to hug me too, but he just looked down at me and nodded his head slowly. I do not know what we were agreeing to, but I nodded my head the same way. He turned and went back to the back of the line. Someone started clapping and a few people patted him on the back. I did not know at the time, but later on, Mother explained it to me.

"Retard is a very bad word," she told me, "Especially since it doesn't apply to you. You must never let anyone get away with calling you that."

When the soldier called that word, I thought back to Mother telling me to never let anyone get away with that. I stepped in to close the distance and to get inside his effective range like Mike taught me. I struck his ribs with my left fist and with my right, punched him in the solar plexus. He made a loud 'OOOF' sound and he tried to grab me. I could see his shoulders moving before his arms did so I dropped down low before he could get a hold of me. I rolled behind him and kicked at the back of his left knee. He dropped to one knee and tried to grab me again. I punched at the back of his hand and he drew it back with his face all scrunched up. I was about to kick him in the jaw. With him down on his knees, his head was in the perfect spot for this type of blow and it would have knocked him unconscious. I saw Mike and Ian running toward us so I did not kick the soldier. He made one last attempt to strike me with a hook punch, but he was very slow so I dodged out of the way and backed up two steps. Ian said that two steps is the universal sign for 'don't keep coming if you don't want to get messed up.'

Mike was yelling at the soldier, "What the hell is going on here?!"

The soldier stuttered, I think he was trying to explain without getting in trouble. Ian came directly to me.

"You okay, William?"

I told him, "Yes. I am fine. He called me a bad word and my

mother said I should never let anyone get away with that."

Ian looked back over his shoulder at Mike and they made a face at each other. Ian and I went back to the fence for our patrol and Mike walked away with the soldier I had just beaten up.

So, Ian said I have to stay here with Mike. Mike said he will continue to train me while Ian is gone. I will also continue to do my jobs around the compound. Mike has said that he will let me be tower guard since I am a very good shot. I told Ian not to worry, that I would make him proud. He reached out to shake my hand. I do not like people to touch me, but Ian is different. Ian is my friend, so I shook his hand. I think I did it right.

Then Ian and the others got into their trucks and left through the gate. I started the stopwatch feature on my wristwatch to count the time he was gone.

12

Garett

Mick smoothed things over the best he could after I beat the shit out of that mouthy son of a bitch. He knew well enough to leave Emma alone. That may not be totally true, because I refused to let her leave my side after that. It could have been that he wasn't in the mood to get another ass-whooping. Aunt Amy wouldn't let us go very far either. She told me that I had to always be on the lookout for the signal that we were out of there. I didn't really understand why we couldn't just leave now.

Zoe was making lists again. That was a good sign. At least the plan wasn't all talk. I am more than ready to move on. We have our own copy of the map now, "just in case we get separated from the rest of the group." Our caravan had grown so much that it wasn't a big stretch of the imagination to see that was a possibility. Grabbing stuff on the road was never a problem before, I don't get why we suddenly have to be so cautious.

"I am not having this conversation with you again, Garett." Aunt Amy had a way of making me feel like I was five years old. "Winter is coming soon enough and I worry that we have gotten so used to other people taking care of some of the important things, we could end up dying of something stupid like frostbite."

"We each have all the snow gear you could come up with."

"You know what I mean, Garett. I wasn't being entirely literal, and you know it. I swear sometimes you just like to push my buttons." I had a way of making Aunt Amy talk like she was a teenager.

She wasn't my mom but ever since we left home, she might as well be. Of course, I was grateful to her, but it was hard to tell her that. Even after what happened to Hannah. There wasn't anything that could have been done to stop us from losing her. Some days, though, I'm glad she's gone. Not because I don't want her around, but the world is so screwed up and scary, and she was so little. No kid should spend their childhood being chased around by monsters that want to eat you or people who want to kill you and steal your stuff.

"Sorry," I said, hoping not to sound sarcastic.

"Whatever," she snorted.

I had obviously failed at doing so.

She headed over towards Mick. She was always heading over to Mick, especially when I tick her off. I guess I shouldn't be upset. He is a nice enough guy, but it has always grated my nerves that he just showed up and was able to weasel his way into being with her. Something was just too convenient about the whole thing. After what happened with that asshole over Emma, though, being with Mick might be the best thing that could have happened. The other guys in the group seemed to know enough to keep away from her out of fear that they might piss him off.

My truck was positioned right behind the sweet ride that Mick had managed to get during our last run. It was cherry red and in perfect condition, a garage-kept beauty with intricately detailed flames running up the hood. Someone had loved her before the outbreak, but their love would never compare to the affection that Mick had for the truck. He went on and on for two full days about it being his dream ride and how in all his years, he never believed he would own a piece of machinery as fine as that one.

I saw the draw of a tricked-out truck, but with Mick, it was borderline obsession. Aunt Amy says it's normal but I can't imagine allowing myself to become that attached to a vehicle. As it is, we're lucky if we get to keep the same one for more than a few months, and it always seems to be the clunkers that make it that long. The nice vehicles are cursed. They're too nice to exist for too long in this crappy-ass world.

As we pulled away for our slow crawl toward the next campsite, I looked over at Emma and ran my fingers along her legs. Tracing circles on her thigh had a calming effect on me. I hadn't realized how on edge I really was until we started to pull away and my fingers on my left hand began to ache from my grip around the steering wheel. I began to daydream about what it would feel like to finally hit the open road.

All I had ever known of driving was the stop-and-go snail's pace that we were forced to keep as we went from one supply run to the next. It was going to be amazing to finally be able to put the pedal all the way down to the floor for the first time ever.

"Garett! The road!" Emma shouted, panicked, from the seat next to me.

"Shit!" I almost rear-ended Mick's brand-new beauty. "Sorry,

Em."

"What were you thinking about? You really zoned out there." She looked concerned, and slightly frightened. I guess almost smashing into the back of a pickup truck will do that to you.

"Nothing. Just how much I want to leave this group of losers behind. I don't know how many more times I can sit in this line of cars and drag ass down the road. We used to cover so much ground when it was just the five of us. Now, most days, I think we are just going around in a circle."

"Yeah," Emma looked sadder than I had seen her in a long time.

"You know you are one of us now, right? Aunt Amy said so."

"I know. I was just thinking how hard it was for just Dad and me until we found this group. I miss him. But I guess it isn't realistic to think people will live forever anymore."

"Damn, Em. When did you get so cynical?"

"Not cynical, realistic. I don't know how much more loss I can take. So, instead of having it come up out of nowhere and catch me off guard, I decided to start expecting it. That way if any of us wake up tomorrow, I'm pleasantly surprised."

"Damn, Em. Just, damn."

The caravan was giving the signal for "All stop". I smacked the steering wheel out of frustration. My brain couldn't handle another day of mindlessly wandering through stores and houses looking for the next great treasure. This time had a different feel to it. The others didn't jump out of their cars and trucks to head off on the next scouting party. It was eerily still for a few minutes.

Mick began flashing his brake lights at me. Five fast flashes followed by a pause. Over and over again, he sent the signal. It didn't register at first. It had been so long since we had run into trouble on the roadway. But there we were, sending the five-flash code. We had made the mistake of hitting a horde. I remembered that I was supposed to be passing the signal back.

I put the truck in park and gave the brakes five quick pumps, then counted to five. Five quick pump and wait, pump and wait. Whoever had taken the lead this morning had made too many mistakes for all of us to get out of this mess. We were blocked in from all sides. The horde was in front of us and the caravan was lined up neatly behind us. The lead car had led us into a bottleneck, something that we usually avoided at all costs for just this reason.

The signal had to work its way to the back, and hopefully those cars would get out of our way before we were overtaken by the massive parade of death. The hordes were growing larger by the day, like drops of water pooling with each other. They were so massive that the only chance you had was to head in the opposite direction as quickly and silently as possible. I was trying to do a headcount of the cars behind us when the RV that had been directly following me started to back up. I used that gap to turn my truck around and hoped that Mick would be able to follow suit.

Shots rang out from the front of the line. The only reason they would be firing is if their car had been breached. The RV was moving as fast as old Dan could manage, but it wasn't fast enough to get away from the hungry zombies. As soon as I saw a hole, I sped around him and tore ass away from the line of cars. This had to be our moment. Aunt Amy couldn't expect us to try to save all those people from being overrun.

"Hold on!" I shouted to Emma.

The needle climbed higher on the speedometer, and my heartbeat raced to match it. Emma had the 'oh shit' handle in a death grip. Fifty, sixty, seventy. I rolled the windows down so I could feel the air whip through my hair.

"Garett! Slow down! You are going to kill us!"

"Not until we're safe, Em!" I yelled back at her, but not out of terror, more out of excitement.

"That'll never happen if you wrap us around a tree!" She screeched.

Eighty, ninety, a hundred. The needle began to shake as it passed into triple digits. I pulled back off the gas and allowed the car to drift back down to a safer speed. Fifty was still far faster than I had been able to go when restricted by the rules of the preppers. Safety first. Slowly and surely. Never stop being aware of the dangers around you.

Someone must have forgot that last one. That was how we ended up speeding away from a situation that would have been easily avoided if those steering the ship had thought enough to allow all the cars an easy exit. I had been driving for over a half an hour before I realized no one was following behind us.

"We need to pull over and wait for Mick," I told Emma.

"What if they don't come?"

"Don't be ridiculous. They were right in front of us. We got out and I have way less driving experience than Mick. He could run circles around me." I needed to believe they were coming.

I pulled the truck into the parking lot of a rest stop that was reminiscent of the one we were living on the roof of when the preppers first found us. I pulled a ladder out of the back of the truck and made my way up to the rooftop. Emma followed quickly behind me, carrying her bag filled with essentials. The high ground would keep us safe if the horde was following behind us and we would be able to see the rest of our family when they made their way down the highway.

I wasn't sure if they would know to stop at the rest stop, so did my best to mark it for them. I parked the truck in a spot that would be easy to spot from the road. Emma and I hung towels down from the roof in hopes that they would see the familiar colors and know we were there. Mostly, I hoped they would have the same sense of nostalgia when they saw it, and hopefully that would lead them to at least check it out.

Hours passed, and nothing. I couldn't allow myself the thought that we lost them all. They had to be alive. As darkness fell, I looked at the stocked campsite we had on the roof and wished I could thank Aunt Amy for making me prepare for this moment. Emma and I would spend the evening warm and comfortable physically while losing it mentally. I did my best to hold it together for her but as we curled up together in the sleeping bag, a feeling of guilt set in.

Maybe I had wished for freedom a little too hard, while never really considering what it might cost.

13

Ian

Our route south took us around most of the heavily populated areas. I knew enough from my trip north with William to avoid anywhere that used to be civilization and to stick, instead, to back roads, backwoods, and bumfuck rural areas. We made surprisingly good time getting out of New Jersey. The only real contact we ran into on the way out of the state came in the form of a small group pretending to be raiders.

We knew they were there, waiting just past a bridge abutment. I radioed back to the other two vehicles and alerted my crew. As we passed under the bridge, they came charging out from the tree line. If I had wanted to, I could have driven through them, but curiosity got the best of me and I rolled the Humvee to a stop. They drew handguns and a couple of hunting rifles on us and some scruffy looking old guy in a leather jacket made his way toward my window. Out of the corner of my eye, I noticed Ken stiffening and gestured for him to relax.

"Afternoon fellas," I said cheerfully, rolling down my window. "Lovely day for a drive. Always wanted to visit the Jersey Shore. Any of you know where I could get some salt water taffy?"

Leather Jacket did not seem to appreciate my humor. "Who are you, where did you come from, and where are you going?"

"That's a lot of questions," I replied. "Suppose I don't feel like answering them?"

He smiled, "Then my men will put lots of messy holes in you and your friends."

I shook my head. "Don't see that happening." I flipped the signal switch on my radio and in one smooth motion, the twelve men from the other vehicles poured into view, weapons drawn. Leather Jacket flinched. The two men in the road in front of me looked nervously from around their little toy rifles at the military hardware my guys were packing. "Look," I said, really wanting to defuse the situation, "neither one of us wants a firefight. Even though your guys will be wiped out, I still stand to lose at least a couple of men, and I can't have that. So get the fuck out of our way and we'll part company. What say?"

Leather Jacket actually seemed to ponder it for a moment, like he was weighing the odds that he would be one of the lucky few to walk away from this if it went down. Then he threw up a hand signal and his men lowered their weapons.

"Much obliged," I said, putting the Humvee into gear. Just like that we were on our way again, barely a ten-minute rest stop. I wasn't fool enough to believe all our encounters would play out the same way, but a win's a win.

We crossed into Delaware and made our way due west as soon as we were across the river. I got word that one of the trucks needed to refuel so we stopped at the next strip mall we saw. We didn't need to check the cars scattered around. We made straight for the luncheonette at the end of the long arm of the L-shaped complex.

Vick rigged all the diesels to run on fryer oil, we'd be good to go as long as it didn't get too cold. And as an extra added bonus, our convoy left a fragrant trail of french fries.

A quick scan of the area showed no immediate danger, though that didn't mean there wasn't any lurking behind the plate glass windows. I sent three men into the luncheonette to retrieve the oil while the rest of us tended to securing the perimeter. I told Ken to stay in the truck, he looked ecstatic at the idea.

Most of the stores had been looted already. The electronics place looked like a bomb went off inside. I never understood that. The world is ending, what the hell are you going to do with a big screen TV or a high-end set of stereo speakers? Two guys signaled a contact in the pharmacy. I made my way over and saw three of them shuffling around the back of the store. They hadn't seen us yet so I motioned everyone to stay to the side of the busted-out window. There was no way of knowing how many of them were milling around back there. It was too dark to get an accurate count and I didn't want to risk a firefight and possibly draw a swarm.

As we scanned the inside of the darkened storefront, I caught movement out of the corner of my eye and turned to see a small shape disappear around the corner of the short arm of the building, moving way too fast to be one of the dead. I signaled Ranger to follow me quietly and we made our way around to an alley. An overturned dumpster lay against the far wall at the back. Whoever it was had either used the dumpster to vault over the wall into the woods, or was hiding inside it. I moved slowly down the alley with my weapon at low ready just in case. I gave a tap to the dumpster and called out softly, "We ain't gonna hurt you kid. Come on out."

I stood there for a minute waiting and called out again,

"Come on out. We've got food if you're hungry, water if you need it, too." Again, I waited a minute. I didn't want to spook the kid, especially if he was feral or something. I heard a rustling from the other side of the wall and I felt like an ass for a second. Standing here talking to a garbage can. I jumped up on the dumpster and peered over the edge and there he was. Looked like he was maybe ten or twelve, but I couldn't be sure. He was filthy and his clothes were rags. Lucky, I saw him running earlier or I might have confused him for a dragger.

I leaned over the edge a little and practically cooed to the kid, "Come on little one. You shouldn't be out here by yourself. Let's get you something to eat." I had flashbacks to when I first met William. Only this kid didn't have a calm, figuring-shit-out look on his face. He was blank, but like he was figuring whether to fight, fuck, hit the fence. You could still sort of see the little boy in there, but there was something else on top of it.

All of the sudden, he grunted and lunged at me, jumping to try and slash me with a butcher knife I hadn't even seen him holding. I jerked back and almost fell off the damn dumpster.

Ranger called to me from the mouth of the alley, "What the fuck!? You alright?!" He started toward me at a trot and I motioned him back. I leaned back over the wall, more cautiously than last time, but the kid was gone. I scanned the woods, but couldn't see any indication of where he went. I was about to hop the wall and go after him anyway when I heard a scream from the front of the building. Ranger turned and took off around the corner, I wasn't far behind him.

Steve had, for some unknown reason, decided to head into the pharmacy. Guess that's what I get for couching it more like a suggestion than an order. At any rate, he was staggering away from the window holding his neck. Blood spurted from between his fingers, spraying Ranger as he tried to get ahold of him. Ken had jumped out of the Humvee and was trying to help Ranger get Steve on the ground. I hopped through the busted window to find the three we had seen earlier joined by four more tearing Jason apart on the floor. I let out a whistle to signal the others that it was time to haul ass.

Immediately, the three I had sent for the oil came out of the diner each carrying two big five-gallon jugs. One of them had tied a cook's apron into a satchel and had filled it with bread and some cans. Ranger had Steve on the ground and was trying to give him a sedative, but Steve was thrashing and spraying blood everywhere. My whistle also alerted the draggers in the store that a fresh meal had been delivered. They turned from Jason's mangled body and came at me. These guys were old dead. You could tell by the way they moved. Zombies were by no means quick, even the freshest ones had little to no coordination, but these guys moved like they had just come out of a Romero movie. This also meant they would go down easy. The older bones started to rot and crunched a lot easier. I leaned my rifle against the wall and pulled Cappy from the sling on my back. I moved on the closest one and brought the crowbar down on top of its skull, careful to land with the back of the curved end. No sense in getting my favorite weapon stuck in one corpse when I had six others to deal with. And dealt with them I did. By the time Ranger and the others made their way inside the pharmacy, all seven corpses lay on the floor, the last one still twitching. I barely broke a sweat. The nice thing about being immune is that you really don't have worry about the bites and scratches that keep other guys at a distance.

Ranger looked at me, "Steve's dead."

"I figured. You take care of him?"

Ranger nodded solemnly, "It was the only thing I could do for him. His throat had been completely torn out. There wasn't anything else could be done." We all nodded solemnly then. "What about that kid? You still want to go after him?" Ranger added after a moment.

I shrugged. I was legitimately torn. I didn't want to risk losing any more men, especially so early in the mission, but could I really just leave some kid out here on his own.

Ranger caught wind of my hesitation, "Make the call, Boss. I'll back you either way."

I stared off into the woods for almost a minute, but finally I told everybody to load up, we couldn't take the risk. As we drove away, and I know this was just my mind playing tricks on me, I kept seeing that kid in my rearview, only he kind of looked like William.

14

Amy

"Shit, shit, shit!" Mick had a way with words.

He had managed to get the truck turned around just in time to see Garett and Emma pulling past the RV that was now blocking our way to them. Those campers were great for storage and for giving you the illusion of having a safe place to sleep, but they were horrible in a situation like the one we all found ourselves in. They were beasts to maneuver and accelerating quickly wasn't exactly an option you could add on to something that big.

"Zoe, turn around and tell me when the horde comes into sight."

She flipped around towards the back window and let out a screech.

"I will take that to mean now. Shit, shit, shit!"

"Mick, the kids are getting further away. We need to catch up with them now," I pleaded.

"Amy, I know, but right now we need to get out of this God damned mess! Garett was right, we should have left these a-holes a while ago. They've gotten sloppy and all these newcomers aren't trained for these situations. Maybe if we didn't pick up so many strays..." He shot me a look of death, "and don't you for a second say we were strays once, too. We weren't incompetent. These people are going to get us all killed, if they haven't already."

"Mick!" I screamed.

"Wha...." He couldn't finish that question. We slammed head first into the RV. Mick looked away at just the wrong time as the camper had gotten itself wedged into a position on the road where there were too many abandoned vehicles to navigate through and had to come to a dead stop.

"Zoe? Zoe, are you OK?"

She nodded her head at me but I could see from her expression that she was in pain. She hadn't been wearing her seatbelt, and was facing backwards when we smashed into the camper. That led her to bounce off the seats and supply boxes. We didn't really have time to assess her condition, though. The dead were closing in and we needed to get out of their reach before we could check on anyone's injuries.

"I'm going to try and get her moving again," Mick tried to reassure me, but his words were slurred and I knew that was a bad sign.

"Take it slow."

"I don't think we have that luxury," he observed.

It took several minutes to get the truck to unhook itself from the camper, and even then, a large chunk of sheet metal and Styrofoam from the camper was still attached to the grill of our truck as we backed away. The dead had surrounded us on all sides. They quickly swarmed the camper. There was no time to think about staying and helping any of the other vehicles. It was every man for themselves. Screams ripped through the air as we tore away down the road but I didn't have it in me to feel bad.

There was just so much death. It lay like a thick blanket across the landscape. Whenever another body was added to the pile, it became a bit more difficult to see much of a difference. We had all begun to have dead eyes anyway. All I could focus on was the five of us in my little family. We were now separated from two of them, and that fact had my anxiety at a peak level.

Mick was trying to control the truck as the horde caught up to our position and surrounded us, but the front axle had sustained some damage from the run in with the RV. Each swerve and pull dragged a few undead square under the wheels. All that did was make the truck harder to control. Mick, in a last-ditch effort, hit the gas hard enough to pull ahead of the pack but, in the end, all that happened was a peel-out on dead flesh. Suddenly, the truck gained traction and shot forward, sending us flying straight into a brick building façade.

That was the end of the beautiful garage-kept beast. The noise from the impact attracted the attention of a wave of undead that were shuffling along nearby. We had already been in a position where there were too many to fight. Now, with the added attention, we were stuck in a broken car that the zombies would be able to break into by their sheer weight alone. The busted windows would never hold against them.

I looked back at Zoe and was grateful to see that, while she looked stunned, she was conscious. We were going to need to move, and fast, so I needed to know if she was going to be able to get herself out of the car or if it would be up to Mick or me. What I had failed to see was whether Mick would even be up to the job. I was so accustomed to him seeming invincible in situations like this that it had never occurred to me that he could be injured.

I scanned the area for the most logical escape route once we broke the windows. Each step would need to be planned and executed perfectly if we were going to have a shot at getting out of the truck alive. Unbeknownst to me, while I was babbling off my step by step plan, only one of the other occupants of the car could hear me.

"... Then, if, by the grace of God, the door is unlocked, we can head into that brick office building over there. But we need to do it right. Sound good?"

Zoe made a sound that almost sounded like agreement but Mick said nothing.

"Mick? What do you think?" I asked as I continued facing the window, assessing the route one more time.

Nothing.

"Mick? MICK?" I turned my head a little too fast for someone who had just been in two car accidents.

That was when I saw that he was knocked unconscious by the crash. At least, I hoped he was just unconscious. My hand shook as I reached over to check if there was breath coming out of his nose. Thankfully, there was. As happy as I was that he was still alive, however, I now had a very big problem. There was no way I could carry Mick to safety. Even with Zoe's help, which I was pretty sure I couldn't count on, we would not be able to get him from the truck to the building.

"Zoe, are you going to be able to run? I need to know if there is anything wrong with your legs. We are going to have to get out of this truck soon." My voice trailed off. She wasn't answering and I had no idea what we were going to do. There was a good chance that this was the end of all of our stories. The dead were slamming against the glass, cracking the already broken glass a bit more with each push.

The world slowed to a snail's pace. The last few months played out before me. The initial outbreak. My brother attacking his wife. The kids and I hiding in my house while the world burned around us. The luck of us finding Mick, and then the preppers. Losing Hannah. Emma and Garett falling for each other. Even the punch that should have ended our time with the group. Instead, I was stubborn and scared. We should have walked away a long time ago. Now, my fear had put us in this situation. We would have been long gone if I could have just let go and moved on.

It was obvious for months, even before the punch, that this group had lost its way. They were unable to make any real progress, and the cold was coming. The kind of cold that we, as modern Americans, have not known since the invention of indoor heating. We were going to freeze and no one seemed concerned about it. Instead, the preppers spent day after day playing class president and ordering each other around for the sake of fairness. This led to an inexperienced person being in charge, and that had led everyone right into a death trap.

I pushed Mick carefully. I was afraid his injuries would get worse if I shook him too hard, but I needed him to wake up. It was in that moment that I realized how much I depended on his judgement. I had allowed it to replace my own in many situations and I had become soft because of it. He groaned but was unable to gain any real consciousness. Instead, he mimicked the sound of the zombies that were trying their damnedest to break through the glass that separated them from their next meal.

I surveyed the area one more time and realized there wasn't a chance in Hell that we would be able to get through the mob surrounding us right now even if we were in tip top condition, which we were not. Zoe was holding her head and staring blankly out the window next to her. She didn't even look scared, and for that, I was sad. This was a horrible world to grow up in. The young ones had lost more than their innocence. They had lost their will to live because they knew this life was temporary. Our existence here was temporary and they were just barely hanging on with no real fight in them.

"Zoe, I need you to help me roll Mick over to my seat."

She didn't respond.

"Zoe!" That got her attention.

"Uh huh." She nodded, not quite fully there.

"I need you to help me roll Mick to my seat. We need to be careful in case he hurt his neck."

"Why?"

"What do you mean 'Why?' We need to try to move the truck, even if it is a little bit. Maybe I can drift it over near the brick building. We're too far away to make it now. We waited too long." I pleaded.

"What's the point?" She asked as she turned towards the monsters chomping at her through the glass.

"To live, Zoe! The point is to live!"

"Why? We are just going to end up here again. Aren't you tired of it? I am. I'm so tired. Maybe if I take a nap, I'll feel better." She murmured as she lay her head down on the seat.

There was a bit of blood trickling out of her ear. I may not be a doctor, but I know a head injury when I see one. Damn it. She had a concussion, and the worst thing for her to do would be to sleep right now. She may never wake again. Now I had two injured people that were unable to move themselves, a horde so big I couldn't count all of them, and a broken truck.

It was a Hail Mary, but if I could just shift Mick over by myself, maybe the truck would bless us with another hundred feet. Just enough to bump us into the wall under the fire escape. The ground level door was out of the question now.

As I pulled him towards me, Mick threw up all over himself and the floor between us. That was probably a bad sign. The smell hit me and I struggled not to heave myself. I gave up on being gentle and pulled as hard as I could, rolling Mick halfway across the seat into what looked like the most uncomfortable position I could've managed to have him land in. It left just enough room for me to squeeze past him and into the driver's seat.

I prayed to the God that my parents had taken me to worship every Sunday, hoping he would remember me even though we haven't ever been that close, and turned the key. The belt shrieked as the truck started, but it sounded as though a bag of wrenches had been thrown into the engine. This only drew more of the dead over to where we were. More prayers, this time out loud, as I slowly backed away from the wall we had smashed into. As the truck lurched inches at a time, it felt like a washing machine with an off-balance load in it. Now, the real test. I shifted into Drive and pushed the gas. Nothing.

"Fuck!"

I slammed my head down on the steering wheel, which was stupid for two reasons. One, it hurt like hell, and two, I landed perfectly on the horn, adding more noise to bring another wave of unwanted attention.

"Damn it, Mick! Get up! I need you to help me think! We are all going to die here and I don't know how to change that!" I screamed at him as I shook him furiously.

Making his injuries worse really wasn't a concern anymore.

We needed a way out and I was unable to find one. There was no way we would all make it out of this situation, and I was seriously beginning to doubt that any of us would still be breathing by tomorrow. The only movement I could get out of the truck was Reverse, so that was going to have to do.

On the back seat where Zoe was curled up, there had been a large pile of supplies in bags and boxes next to her. They had been tossed about a bit from the crashes. Looking at them, the only idea for survival I could come up with that had even the slightest chance of working dawned on me. Sadly, it meant I had to leave one of them out in the open. I may have become numb to the death of acquaintances, but these two were my family. Nothing would ever make this decision alright, but it was the only choice I had.

The zombies were pounding on the windows, seconds away from busting through the cracked glass. No more time to think. There was no time left to do anything but react. I threw the truck in Reverse and hit the gas. We didn't speed off, but we were able to break away from the dead ones that were working their way in through the windows. I got us rolling and, by luck, catching the only break I managed to catch that day, started to roll down a hill.

The truck was rattling and shaking, but it was moving. I let go of the wheel and turned towards the back seat. My landing was awkward but it was perfectly timed. Zoe was so much lighter than Mick as I pulled her down to the floor. Hopefully, my body being wedged above hers between the seats would block the hungry monsters that were sure to break in. Laying across her, I was unable to see what we hit, but it didn't matter anyway. Wherever we landed was where we would make our final stand. I pulled the bags and boxes down over us, leaving

Mick as the only one the horde would see as they broke through into our truck.

I prayed again. This last prayer I whispered over and over.

"Please Lord, let me sleep. Don't make me hear him die. Please Lord. Give me just this one thing."

That prayer went unanswered.

15

Ken

One thing that never got talked about in all those zombie movies and books and TV shows that used to be on is the smell. The smell of dead, rotting flesh is everywhere. Between the bodies everywhere and the zombies themselves, the wind carries the stench of death with every puff of breeze. I guess after a while we got used to it, but it never went away. When we reached the CDC building, we broke through a hastily constructed barricade into the foyer of the CDC building. Ian swears this wasn't here when he left, meaning someone took up residence after he had gone. From the looks of the entry way, there had been a hell of a fight here. Ian pointed out the rotted remains of zombies he himself had killed and estimated that the number of bullet casings on the floor had doubled since he last saw this place. There were fifteen more dead on the floor and several bodies in the stairwell. Ian said those were new too, well not new judging by the decay, but more recent.

Ian led us up the stairwell. "Weapons at the ready guys, it looks like somebody definitely tried to make a home here after

I left. There's no way of telling who, if anybody, is still here."

We moved slowly to the second floor with me in the middle of the group. I had the pistol that Ian had shown me how to use, but I still felt kind of useless. I was impressed with the way these men handled themselves. Some of them had been soldiers before, but even the ones that weren't still acted like they had been their entire lives. As we reached the second-floor landing, Ian signaled for everyone to stop. He and Ranger nodded at each other and took positions on either side of the door. Jacob eased the door open a crack and peered through. After he judged the coast to be clear, he pushed it the rest of the way open. The hallway was empty. Ian moved back into the lead position and we fell in behind him. He used hand signals to direct group of men to check each room. One by one, rooms were cleared and we moved to the back of the building to a row of executive offices.

The rooms had been ransacked. Desks overturned, files scattered, cabinets smashed. Judging from the content I found on the floor, these were administrative offices. I didn't need payroll forms, I needed research. "We need to find the lab," I told Ian.

"Fifth floor was where they were holding me. There's also some rooms in the basement that might have what you want."

Ranger piped in with a groan, "The dark, creepy basement… Great." The rest of the group chuckled nervously.

"Let's check upstairs first while we have the light," Ian said.

We cleared the rest of the floor and moved back to the stairwell and up to the third floor. The men went through the same motion of checking each room and, again, all were empty. This floor held more executive offices, a large cafeteria devoid of food, a small gym, and more bodies. Ian didn't remember if there were more than were here last time. The fourth floor was essentially a barracks. Every locker had been raided and anything of use had been taken. We moved to the fifth floor, where patients had been kept. As the men cleared the rooms, I rifled through papers at the nurses station. I found mostly activity logs, timesheets, takeout menus, nothing of real value. I found charts for the fifteen patients that had resided here, Ian's among them. I stacked the thick binders on a cart and went back to my search. I saw Ian and one of the other men stop outside one of the rooms and overheard Ian say that this was where he was held. They pushed the door open. Ian leaned his head in, scanned, and shrugged. They continued down the hall.

Ian walked over to me, "You find what you need?"

I shook my head, "Some things I can use, but this is all patient data, test results, vital signs. What I need is the actual research data. Maybe that will be downstairs. I'm just hoping it won't all be digital."

"We can always bring a couple computers back to the airport with us, hook them up to the generators."

"I wouldn't know which ones to bring. We would have to bring back the servers and then configure everything. Then there's passwords and encryption… There's no sign of power here, so it's paper or it's worthless."

Ian agreed and resumed his search. I continued to shuffle papers around the nurse's desk in a futile attempt to make what I needed magically appear when I heard a shout from the end of the hall, then gunfire. It was brief, maybe a shot or two, but everyone ran toward its source. I could hear Ian shouting orders as the stairwell door slammed open and several sets of stamping boots entered the hall.

"Get down!" Ian shouted and I obeyed. I dropped to the floor behind the desk and clumsily fumbled the pistol from its holster on my hip. I knew enough to take the safety off and to chamber a round, but if I actually had to fire the thing, I had serious doubts as to my effectiveness.

The gunfire escalated, reached a crescendo, then began to peter off. Finally, like popcorn in a microwave, the last few pops went off and then it was quiet except for the sound of several men groaning. The smell of burnt gunpowder was thick in the air. I didn't dare move until Ian gave me the all-clear. He called out to his men to sound off, which they did. One by one, each affirmed that he was okay. Not one of our side had been hit. Ian called for them to stay put. He made his way back to me and crouched beside me behind the concealment of the desk.

"You okay?" he asked.

I nodded. "Who the hell was that?"

Ian shrugged. "They weren't here when I left. I'm guessing they found the place empty and decided to make a home." He turned to Ranger and three others. "Keep an eye on that door and send three men to watch the other one. Don't go after these guys, but if they come back through, cut them in half." Each man nodded an affirmative. Ian faced me again. "We still have a mission here. No doubt these assholes are just defending themselves. If the opportunity arises, I'll let them know that we aren't a threat if they leave us alone, but all the same, I'm not taking any chances. Keep looking through this shit and when you are ready, we'll move down to the basement where the labs are." I nodded as Ian got up and moved toward the bodies of the men he had killed. "We leave the weapons and ammo," he called out to the men, "As of right now, these people are not the enemy. If they come at us again, that's a different story, but no one is to engage without my say-so. Understood?"

Each man sounded a yes, or some variation thereof, and I continued to dig through the now even more scattered papers around the nurse's desk. After settling on Ian's file, it was the only one I would have any context for, I told Ian I was ready to move on. We formed a column with me in the middle and Ranger at the back as Ian lead us down the stairwell toward the lab. We didn't see anyone else on the way down, and I don't think we were followed.

16

William

I do not understand why people act the way they do. They can be so rude. I was walking with Mike along the double fence that separated us from the road when an alarm sounded over his radio. I did not have my radio with me. I didn't need to carry a radio when I was with Mike and it would waste batteries anyway.

Mike screamed "REPORT!" into his radio and whoever answered talked so fast that I could not understand him. Ian says that when you talk into a radio you have to be de-lib-er-ate with your words so the other person can understand you. This person was not being de-lib-er-ate so I could not tell what he was saying. Mike seemed to get mad. I think it was a mad face. His eyebrows got all wrinkled and the corners of his mouth pointed toward the ground. I tried my best to make my face look the same.

When the man in the radio stopped talking, Mike pushed the special red button on the side of his radio and yelled, "All teams to firing positions! Human contact at gate 3!" Gate 3 was close to where we were. Mike started to run toward Gate

3 so I followed. Mike unslung his rifle, so I did too.

"William, I want you to go back to the main house, to the special room I showed you, okay?"

I shook my head. The special room was where all the children and old people were supposed to hide if there was ever trouble. I did not want to hide with the children and the old people. "I am a soldier, sir. I want to stay and fight." I knew it was not correct to disobey a direct order. Ian said that was one of the worst things a soldier could do. I did not want to hide. I wanted to fight.

Mike made another face I didn't understand and said, "Alright. But you stay close to me. And don't get shot."

I nodded and moved behind Mike as we ran up to the fence were the people were. There were three cars in the road that led to the gate. Standing at the gate there were three men. There were ten women and three children in the cars that I could see. They all had their hands in the air. I think they looked scared. I heard Mike yell to the men in the tower to keep their weapons ready, then he spoke to the first man in the group.

"Lay your weapons on the ground and step back. Then we can have a civilized conversation," he said.

The man responded by nodding his head. He and the rest of them laid their guns and knives down. "We're just looking for somewhere safe. We don't want any trouble."

"Where did you come from?" Mike asked.

"North. Not too far, maybe forty or fifty miles. We escaped from Long Beach Island. They've got the island sealed off and pretty well defended, but the guy running the show there is a total psycho."

Mike turned to me and whispered real soft in my ear, "I want you to walk back to where the mill is. When you get there move out to the fence line and come back this way. Don't let anybody see you. See if you can see other people out in the treeline. Report back to me. Do not engage if you see anyone, just tell me."

I nodded slowly and gave an affirmative because Ian told me that you always give a verbal confirmation of an order. I was happy because Mike had given me a real job to do, not just following him around or some silly kid stuff. I could hear Mike talking to the men as I moved back to the spot where he told to go. I made my way out toward the fence. I gathered up some branches and leaves and made my camouflage. Mike and Ian both said I was really good at camouflage. I like camouflage. If no one can see me, I do not have to worry about interacting with them.

I moved slowly along the fence. It doesn't make sense to move fast when you are camouflaged. Trees and bushes don't move fast or even at all. If someone sees a bush or dirt pile moving at all they will know something is going on. So, I moved slow. Move. Stop. Watch. Move. It takes a long time to cover ground this way, but you have to go slow to be effective.

I did not see anyone in the woods, or on the road which Mike did not tell me to check, but I checked anyway. I did not know if he wanted me to stay camouflaged all the way back to his position so I stopped where I was and waited. I could see the group of them standing on the other side of the fence, but I could not hear them very well. I moved just little closer so that I could hear the words they were saying. I decided to keep a firing position on them just in case. I thought that Ian would have done the same thing.

The men were pleading with Mike to let them in. Mike waved forward a team of men to gather their weapons and check them for bite marks or scratches. After a thumbs-up, the gate was opened and the cars rolled through. I went to Mike to give my sitrep because after a mission you always give a sitrep. I told Mike everything I saw and he said that I did good. It made me happy that Mike said that. I wanted Ian to come back so he could see that I was a good soldier.

Mike was talking to the people that had come through the gate. He was asking them about where they came from. Apparently, they snuck away from an island because "Vincent is crazy". I don't know who Vincent is, but if he was crazy, it is good that these people got away from him. Mike continued to ask them questions. How many were on the island, how had they gotten away, were Vincent or his men looking for them. As he talked to them, his tone of voice was friendly but his face did not match.

As soon as he was done asking them questions and they were led to a quarantine bunkhouse, Mike took out his notebook and began writing in it. I knew that he was writing down what the people had told him in response to his questions.

I waited for him to stop writing and asked, "Do you think we need to be concerned with Vincent?"

Mike looked sideways at me, I think he was making a surprised face. "Not sure, William. We knew that this island was there and that there might be people on it, but we haven't been able to make any contact with them so we figured they were either dead or undead. It might be a good idea to send a couple scouts to see what's what, but I'm not guessing these people are any kind of advance party or anything. What's your take, William?"

I felt good that he asked me what I thought. I told him that they looked really scared, not just pretending to be scared.

I can usually tell if people are pretending, like when Mike's face didn't match with his words. I told him that if they were trying to spy on us for this Vincent person, they might really be scared so they could still be lying. I told him that if Vincent were really crazy, he might send people after the ones who showed up. If they really escaped. I told him that I thought we should maintain suspicious awareness. Ian had told me this phrase a few times. It means to keep your eyes open and pay attention to what's happening.

Mike nodded his head in agreement. "Reminds me of an old quote, 'Be polite. Be professional. But have a plan to kill everyone you meet.'" Then he moved like he was going to pat me on the shoulder, but I flinched out of the way.

"Sorry, kid. Forgot. You did really good today and I'm glad to have you around."

17

Vincent

There are rumblings of a mutiny. I'm beginning to wonder if they need to have a refresher course to remind them who's in charge of things. Our calling here comes from above, and if they're not going to be part of the that, then they can be tossed out to the dead. We have managed to clear the island twice now. You would think that having an island paradise free from the flesh-eating monsters would be enough for them.

It isn't though, and the more comfortable they become, the more freedom they want. Freedom is what let the dead get back on this island again. Freedom is how they ended up begging at my feet to be saved. There is no freedom in this new world. I am the king, and they are my subjects. I wish Jessica was still here. She understood our calling. She wasn't weak like these other women I was forced to deal with now.

In the aftermath of the redistricting effort, we managed to find two other women who were immune to the bite of the undead. While not surprising to me, this came as a complete shock to Art. He's taken over the job of documenting the glory of my reign. This honor has allowed him the privilege of shadowing me and keeping record. He had been a newspaper man in the old days, so this seemed like the best way for him to be able to do his new job. While I enjoyed my time conversing with Jessica, Art has the personality of a stump. It became painfully clear from the first few days that he should fade into the background.

He stood there slack jawed when two weeks after the wall being moved two familiar couples came crying towards our camp. Everyone was sure that they had all perished or left the island, but there stood two men trying in vain to protect their women from the monsters they were facing. I was going to have them shot, but then they were yelling about immunity and bites. I knew it would only be the women. No other men were touched by greatness, and once their stories were confirmed, we led the women to my home. Protests were made about staying together. I made sure they understood that the men being allowed back inside was a gift of my kind nature, not something they should take for granted.

The two blessed women were overjoyed with their position in our group as they with showered with all the gifts their hearts desired. It was a shame, but one of them had a husband who was unable to see that the importance of our mission overrode their exchanged vows. The world was a far different place when they wore those fancy outfits and stood at the front of what is now quite possibly a defunct religious institution, swearing monogamy to an outdated deity and the state. His wife knew that her place was with me.

I tried to be lenient at first, merely locking him away until he could see the error in his ways. After two escapes, during the last of which he had made it all the way to the room where the women were kept, he had to be put down. It was for the best, though. Once he was gone, his wife could finally be free of the old life that still bound her and give herself fully to me. Her silence was a wonderful way to show how seriously she toke her duty. The tears of joy dried up after a few days.

Earl, always the worrier, has been scurrying around the camp. His constant negativity began to wear me thin on patience for him. No one wants to hear how the sky is falling every day. Does he celebrate my triumphs? No. He just moves onto the next fire, and stops me from being able to enjoy what should be my greatest accomplishments. I have created a safe zone in chaos, carved out from the darkness stands this beacon of light. It is poetic that our home includes a very large and quite literal beacon of light. The Barnegat lighthouse may not work right now, but one day I will have that light shining to bring more subjects to be safe in my magnanimous arms.

I finally had enough, and sent him to time out to think about how he addresses me. The world will keep turning without him and maybe it was time that he learned that. I on the other hand am not so easily replaced. My mission, my life itself, was our entire reason to get up each day and keep going. Bothering me with trivial issues was a strain on the real task at hand. I looked over at the two women sleeping soundly on the edges of my king-sized bed and wished I had more time to stay with them, but things needed to be done so I could return to them later to try for an heir again.

As I scanned the horizon, Art scribbling furiously in his notebook behind me, I hatched a plan for how to deal with the small group of rabble-rousers who were unable to see my vision and the gift I have given them by allowing them to stay here. The sun was just about to rise above the horizon, the signal for the change of guards and the start of a new day.

We would have to process the new batch of refugees that had arrived last night, and I would need to set the wheels in motion to squash all those seeking to sabotage the safety that we all enjoyed.

The brick-wall brothers appeared behind me like clockwork, tromping through the room with their usual amount of finesse. Another day, another chance to save humanity.

18

Ian

I had no idea what the hell Ken was hoping to find here, but I knew he wasn't finding it. We cleared floor by floor on our way down to the basement, then into the sub-basement where the labs were. I left Ranger and two others to watch the stairwell in case our new friends decided to follow us down here. With a couple of theirs down, not knowing how many there were, I figured they'd leave us be for the time being, but I wasn't taking the chance of getting trapped down here.

Every room we came to looked about the same, there wasn't much in the way of carnage down here. It looked more like people had just shut down for the day and never came back. Ken got more antsy and upset the further down the line we got. He kept mumbling something about damned EMR's. I have no idea what an "EMR" is, but apparently, they were making it hard for him to find what he needed.

"It's all in the damned, useless computers!" he yelled, slamming the door on another file cabinet. "There's plenty of patient info on paper, but no real data. This is such a waste."

I put a hand on his shoulder, trying to be consoling I guess,

"What if we drag a few of them back with us, maybe, we can get them working back at the base."

He shrugged dejectedly and slumped in a chair rubbing his temples.

I pressed further, "There's power here. We could plug a few in to the emergency outlets and see which ones have what you need. Then we throw them in the Humvee and cart 'em back. You can nerd out on the data all you want back home."

Ken's eyes brightened a little. "I don't know if they'll work without a network to connect to, but we can at least see what was stored locally on the hard drives."

"We'll have to get the generator running again. It's in the garage where I stole my first Jeep from." I thought back wistfully, well not wistfully, but you know, kind of nostalgic in a way, to that time last year when I first busted out of here. "We'll need two guys on the door here and three to come with us to the garage. I want two men on guard duty at the genny just in case. I don't think those guys will show themselves again, but one or two of them might get an idea to take a couple pot shots if we start the power up again." I gathered my men and relayed the plan. I told the few others to gather all the computers into one of the offices, the one that had a bright red outlet on the wall. I knew enough to know that that was an emergency power supply and would get juice from the generator.

We didn't see anyone as we moved up the stairs and across the building to the garage. The lock on the fence surrounding the generator was still intact too. It had run out of fuel. Either the people who had taken up residence in the building didn't realize it was here or were too dumb to realize that they had a huge reserve of fuel in all these vehicles. I knew that at least a few of the gas tanks would be no good. They would either be near empty or the gas would have jellied after all this time, but there should be some usable gas in there somewhere.

Turns out, we didn't even have to check the cars. There were three big, old fifty-gallon drums already hooked up the generator. I found a scrap of paper and dipped it into the filler cap of the first tank. I held out and set my lighter to it. It went up in a bright flash.

"That's a good sign, Ken" I said, "Means the gas will still burn. Now all we have to do is get this beast to kick over."

Ken switched between watching me and glancing nervously at the door we came through.

"Relax, Ken. Nobody we don't want to see is going to come through that door. They'd have to get through Ranger and half a dozen other guys to get to you. And even then, they'd have to go through me." That last part sounded so cliché, so action-movie-hero-like coming out of my mouth that I rolled my eyes and apologized. That finally got Ken to grin a little.

I checked the diagram on the side of the starter, squeezed the primer a few times and got both hands around the big pullcord. I yanked the starter once, twice, three times. The big engine coughed and sputtered but refused to catch. I went at it again, nothing. I saw fear and disappointment battle it out on Ken's face and felt frustration wrinkling my own. I tried a third time, then a fourth. I was about to take Cappy to the damn thing, when my own stupidity struck me. I leaned down and flipped the choke to half-way. One more pull and the genny burst into life with a plume of black smoke from the exhaust.

Ken pumped a fist in victory and actually posted up for a high five.

"Don't tell my dad," I said, slapping his hand "He'd never let me live that one down."

We made our way back upstairs and Ken got right to work setting up monitors and computer towers and docking stations and whatever the hell else geeks did when they were getting ready to go to work. He looked like he finally felt he was pulling his weight and I know how good that can feel. I left him to it and went to get some grub. I needed to figure out a watch rotation, what our perimeter would be, whether or not to clear the building or leave those others to themselves, a bunch of logistical shit that always bored the shit out of me. I wasn't going to be any help to Ken anyway and besides, I knew a certain vending machine near the caf that might still be holding onto a Big Texas cinnamon roll or two.

19

Earl

Four walls that seemed closer together every time the sun rose. Vincent, in his infinite wisdom, decided that his biggest problem was not the undercurrent of justified grievances brewing in the group outside, but the fact that I kept telling him about it. Even my loyalty had cracks in it. You can only be a punching bag for so long before you decide enough is enough. The guards brought me food, and depending on their level of contempt for me, extras. One or two of them even risked themselves by sitting and playing a few rounds of cards with me.

You never knew what could set Vincent off, and something as simple as a round of Rummy could end with a bullet to your brain. Books would be slipped on the tray if it was one of my friends, and food would be half eaten if it wasn't. Days passed. Eventually, I lost count of how long he had me locked away. I began to wonder if he would ever let me out.

"Whatcha actually do?" Frank finally asked one night as he passed me my set of cards.

"Told him that there were problems one too many times." I

sighed as I tried to make matches with what sat in my hand.

"Ha! You should have known better! He only likes to hear good stuff. Hell, even then, he wants it exaggerated. Haven't you been around the longest? You would think that you would know that if you managed to stay alive this long." He had a point.

"Yeah, yeah." I said.

"How come he let you live?" Frank asked. I wondered if that was out of survival instinct. I bet they all think I held some secret to keep them alive if Vincent turned on them, too.

"Who knows?" I said, and his face went sour. "It could be anything. It isn't like he is predictable. Well, maybe a bit. I predict he will overreact all the time."

"Geez, Nostradamus. Thanks. That'll help out a lot."

"When's the last time predictions ever helped anyone?" I asked.

We played in silence for a few minutes as we both tried to come up with a way to change the subject. Talking about Vincent for too long can put a cloud of depression and hopelessness over even the sunniest of people. It was difficult to think of anything else when someone had a stranglehold over your life the way our island dictator did.

"You finish the last few books I left you?" he asked breaking the silence.

"Yup!" I exclaimed. "I read them twice!"

Before the zombie apocalypse, I wasn't much of a reader. Nerd stuff wasn't really my thing. But now, we don't have much else in the way of entertainment. I mean, sure, we can crank the generator up and do a movie night on the beach when the natives get too restless, but there aren't any new movies to look forward to, and the fall line up doesn't exist anymore.

So, eventually, you have seen it all, and all that is left is the unturned pages in the library.

"What did you think? If you liked them, the author has a ton of books in that series. I can sneak a few more in at a time. I mean, who knows how long you are going to be locked up in here?" he placed his last card down.

"Has he said anything about when he is letting me out?" And just like that, we were back on Vincent again.

"Nope, but I'm not close with him." He said relieved. "No one has been trying to fit into your spot. You would think that someone would make a powerplay to get his ear before he lets you out, but everyone is so spooked by him that they just stay far away. Well, except his two big bodyguards. They are always around, but I never see them speaking."

"Yeah, they aren't much for words, those two. They really don't have that much going on in between their ears, so I wouldn't worry too much about the two of them trying to replace me. On the other hand, they definitely won't bring him any bad news." I said trailing off.

Going to sleep that night was harder than it should have been. I had nothing to worry about when it came to my position in Vincent's organization. My biggest problem would be if the people ever got fed up with him. I had to find a way for him to see me as loyal, but distance myself enough for the people to let me live if this whole thing ever comes crashing down.

It would probably be best if I could have an escape set up to get off the island just in case. They would have a hard time stringing me up with him if I was gone before they could catch me. That night, I started the detailed plan called *Operation Save My Skin*. Vincent may have a God complex, but since we found others with an immunity, I no longer believed he was a blessing from Heaven. I should have known no God would make a maniac their messiah.

It was another few weeks before Vincent strolled through the door announcing that I was needed for some menial job. "Earl, get up. You need to go on a run." He said as he kicked me awake.

"Shit." I stuttered. "What? Are you really here?"

"Jesus, Earl. Yes. I'm here. Sometimes, you are just so god damned stupid."

"Sorry. I was sleeping, and it's been so long." I stood at attention.

"Don't be so melodramatic. It hasn't been that long. I actually forgot I put you in here." He chuckled.

It took every ounce of my being to smile at him when he said that. All this time, and it wasn't a punishment anymore. It was an oversight. I thought I was his right-hand man, and in all actuality, I was just an errand boy that is forgotten as soon as I leave his sight. Showing how I really felt about it would lead to another month or two locked away, so I put the mask back on and complimented his independence as we walked out of the room. Quickly, I shifted to the run he wanted me to lead.

"What are we looking to find, and how many men am I taking?"

"Men?" he laughed again. "No. You misunderstand. I want you to go find this for me."

"Don't I need backup? Someone to watch my back?"

"Earl. Are you questioning me again?"

My heart dropped, but I put the mask back before he could see my reaction. With what must have looked like a forced smile, I asked him to continue.

"One of my ladies wants chocolate. I think it is an impossible task, but if it stops her from whining, I say we try to get it. And by we, I mean you. Go grab your shit, and head out. This is a top priority task." He said as he waved his arms dismissively at me.

I stared at his back as he sauntered through the street. He was oblivious to the glares of hate that poured off the faces of everyone but his guards. The entire island hated him, and the tipping point would come. It wasn't a matter of if anymore, but of when. Then, I realized the gift he accidentally gave me. If I was sent out alone to the other side of the wall, I would have a chance to start preparing my escape.

The hate and dread I felt was quickly replaced by a feeling of freedom and elation. Maybe, I will head out on the chocolate run and not come back. I wonder if that is how Jessica disappeared. Did she have some way to escape his clutches? It seemed unlikely due to her confinement, but nothing is impossible. I grabbed my gear and headed out into the danger zone with thought of not only my grand plan, but a smile at the possibility that there were others that got out before me. Hope is a powerful thing. It can fill a man with purpose. Vincent almost broke me in that prison, and now he set me free without realizing it.

20

Jeremy

The kid has been with me for about a week now. It is nice to have company. It's even nicer to have company that doesn't bring a bunch of drama with them. I'll take a boy and his dog over a stripper and her admirer any day. The kid is pretty bright for a, well, a kid. He doesn't draw attention to himself, and that dog of his is amazing. They work together without even speaking. It's a sight to see.

We have been working on a system I like to call "Jeremy is bait." Since they're so stealthy, it makes sense for me to draw out the dead and make a bunch of noise, drawing them away from whatever loot we're after. Then, the two of them run in and grab whatever deliciousness isn't spoiled yet, or even better, something that helps keep us safe. They managed to find a handgun and some ammo the other day. I did a very literal, and cringe worthy, happy dance.

The one thing the kid doesn't know is music. That's okay, though. It gives me something to talk about as we head to the fort. I may not be much of a talker normally, but it feels strange to lead some kid I don't know around without at least trying to make him feel like he can trust me. Plus, who else is going to teach him about all things 90's Alternative?

It took a while, but after a few days he finally opened up a bit. "I think we might stick around with you for a while. That okay by you?" He asked out of nowhere.

"Of course. I told you I was happy to have someone around for a bit. It helps that you have a dog. He makes you a lot cooler," I said with a snicker.

"Yeah," he laughed. "He does."

"Look, kid, I figure you two will stay around as long as it's working for you. That works just fine for me. When we get closer to the place on the paper, you can decide if that's where you want to be. If it's not, you two can just take off. I won't tell anyone I ever knew you. You two are more than capable of taking care of yourselves. I know you are just hanging out with me because it works for right now. That's fine by me. I am not really a 'taking care of people' kind of guy." I said as he shook his head.

I could swear that the dog was shaking his head, too. Must have been my imagination. Being on your own for too long can make you a bit nutty.

"We had a group before. Rocky liked it there. They made him homemade food."

"Yeah?" My stomach growled at the idea of a real home-cooked meal. "What made you leave?"

"It just wasn't working for me anymore. The living can be as annoying as the dead," he said as he laughed.

"Tell me about it," I agreed, thinking back to the stripper. One more moment with her and I may have willingly joined the ranks of shuffling monsters.

"I miss video games."

"Me, too kid. Especially Madden," I said as I packed up the contents of yet another car that had run out of gas. We were going to be hoofing it for a while again. I loved that neither of them seemed to mind.

"You know I can drive," he blurted out.

"Well, shit! Why didn't you tell me earlier? I could have been napping more."

"I wasn't sure if I liked you yet."

That made me laugh until tears rolled from the corners of my eyes. I had no idea why I found it that funny, but it was probably because it was unfiltered honesty. I was so tired of dealing with the fake nonsense you always hear when you meet new people. Not with Max, though. That kid kept it real. Rocky stood watch as we gathered the last of our supplies after I was finally able to compose myself again.

We headed off down the road, hugging the side. Throughout this part of New Jersey, there were long stretches of farmland. Along the sides of the road ran drainage ditches, which we would be able to jump into and hide from the living if we kept perfectly still. The dead were a different story, though. Lying flat on the ground in a hole was not exactly the best way to handle them. So far, our best defense has been a good offense.

We decided not to use the gun that Max had found on zombies. Instead, we opted for a much quieter means of dispatching them. We had been lucky so far that the clusters of zombies we had encountered were small and manageable. I didn't want to ruin that streak by shooting off a loud-ass gun and drawing in a crowd that would be too big for the three of us to handle. The gun was there just in case jumping in the ditch didn't work out quite like we hoped it would.

By the end of the night, we had walked far enough to end up

in another middle of nowhere cluster of homes that may or may not be classified as an actual town. They had long been abandoned. We were getting close enough to the sanctuary on the flyer that most of the people who had lived here were likely either there or dead. Max and rocky looked exhausted, but they weren't complaining. I was grateful for that being tired as hell myself.

There were three properties to choose from and each looked equally shitty. I had a sneaking suspicion that this wasn't due to the apocalypse. I would bet they were shitty before the world went to hell. It just happened that the rest of the world managed to catch up with them now. Property values in this portion of the state were never really all that high anyway. They were just far enough away from civilization to be marketable, however, that was more of an asset now.

"Rocky," I said, scratching the dog's head. "You take a sniff around and pick one of them for us to stay in. Preferably nothing infested by zombies. I am way too tired to put up a fight. I just want to eat and go to sleep."

Damned if that dog didn't circle the outside of each house, smelling the ground as he went. I never knew a dog that understood English so fluently, but the longer I hung out with these two the more convinced I was that I was hanging out with a real-life Lassie.

Rocky finished his inspections and then walked up to the door of the smallest of the three homes. It looked intact enough. We might have to spend a few minutes shoring up the windows and doors, but it was good enough for an overnight stay. He sat down in front of the door. I was about to make my way up to open the door when Max grabbed the back of my shirt.

"That means there are dead in there."

"What means there are dead in there?" I asked.

"Rocky and I have a few signals. That is one of them. If he likes a place, he'll go to the door. He scratches at it if it's empty, but if he sits and stares at it there are dead inside."

"Damn. You two are smart. I thought you had some sixth sense shit going on. That makes a lot more sense. I can't believe I didn't pick up on it on my own. You got any other ones I should know?" I was genuinely curious.

"Not right now, maybe later. We need to deal with whatever is in that house before anything else."

"Alright, kid, but you definitely have to tell me. That is too cool," I said as I pulled out my 10-inch hunting knife.

We were going to be in close quarters with this one but it made sense to clear the house completely before we settled in for the night. Max had his hatchet at the ready as I pulled the door open. We both braced for the attack.

Nothing.

"You sure, that was the signal for dead?" I turned to ask.

"Yup." He said and pointed back towards the door.

There was a zombie, but not one that was going to get to us very quickly. It was missing a leg, so it was dragging itself across the floor towards us. As it pulled itself closer, it left a trail of slimy brown goo behind it.

"Maybe we should just pick another place to sleep," I said.

"You afraid of a one-legged zombie? Come on, we have taken on worse, and that is just in the last few days," he shot back.

"It's not that, kid. That thing is disgusting. It's leaving a smelly trail of either shit or blood behind it on the carpet. I bet it's managed to get that mess all over the entire house. I don't want to sleep in there," I argued.

As the thing was pulling itself closer, we could hear what

almost sounded like someone slurping noodles with each pull. I started to dry heave. Thank god for small miracles, like not having eaten dinner yet. Max was next to me cackling. If the dog had followed suit, I may have lost it.

"Shut the door!" I yelled between heaves.

"Oh, for god's sake." He rolled his eyes as he moved in and planted the hatchet in the zombie's skull. "All better. We all clear now, boy?"

Rocky barked twice.

"Rocky says it is all clear. I'll go check, just in case. The smell might be messing with his nose. I think he would hear them if there were more, though." His voice trailed off as he used his foot for leverage against the dead man's head to pull the hatchet back out, then headed into the house. Rocky leaped in front of him. They were one hell of a team.

"It's all good in here. Kind of a mess, though. Give me a few minutes. I'll check if there's a mop. You should probably stay out on the porch until I get it aired out a bit."

It took a good fifteen minutes before my head stopped spinning. The kid had managed to clean up enough of the mess to call the place home for one night. He had already set up the small camp stove that we had and was cooking a can of beans and pulled pork in a pot he found in the house. You would think, after losing my nonexistent lunch, that my stomach would be in no condition to handle beans and meat. If you thought that, you would be wrong.

Max kept giggling throughout our meal, and continued pretty much until we went to lay down in the locked-up house. "Thanks for that," he said.

"For what? You did all the work."

"For making me laugh. I don't think I have laughed that hard since I saw my first zombie. Feels like years ago."

"I know how you feel, kid. Glad I could be of service." I yawned and rolled over on the couch so I was facing the wall.

Rocky jumped up on the loveseat with Max. We all went to sleep around the same time, no one staying up to keep watch. A good laugh, a ridiculous scenario, and a long day had bonded us in a way that was unexplainable by words. We were a unit, or family, even if it was just for a while. We were finally comfortable enough with each other to let our guard down. Before I could think too hard about how content I felt, I fell fast asleep.

21

Ranger

It's cool that everybody calls me Ranger. My friends used to call me that. It's also cool that everybody thinks I'm a badass. My friends used to think I was a badass too. We used to hang out in Jimmy's mom's basement. Jimmy called it his apartment, but come on, if your mom is only as far away as a basement door, you live with your parents. So anyway, we used to hang out down there all the time because Jimmy had a sweet movie collection. He pirated everything off the internet. Jimmy called himself a hacker, but seriously, anybody can use BitTorrent. So we would watch movies and smoke pot and talk about what would happen if there was a zombie apocalypse. I said I would get two big .44 magnum revolvers on hip holsters and blast my way through crowds of zombies. Mitch said he would get a crossbow, just like that guy from the TV show. Jimmy would show off this samurai sword he got at the mall and say that was all he would need. We thought we were so badass.

When everything started to go to shit, back even before the news ever got around to reporting what was going on, Mitch called it. He was always on news aggregator sites and he said what was coming. We got all our gear together in Jimmy's mom's basement. I didn't have any guns or anything and Mitch never got around to getting a crossbow, but we had a ton of knives and swords. We thought we were ready. We thought the three of us were gonna save the world. We watched news reports and followed Twitter feeds and talked about what was coming and how much ass we were gonna kick.

The night it started for me, Jimmy's mom came home from work, she worked at the grocery store, and says that there was all kinds of "commotion" downtown that afternoon. That's the word she used, "commotion". What she meant was that some dude got off the crosstown bus, threw up blood all over the street, then died right there in front of the Pack 'n Save. She saw the whole thing from her register. She says that even through the crowd of people she can see the guy on the ground and another guy on top of him trying to do CPR. Only by the time the cops get there, the guy isn't on the ground anymore. He's on his feet attacking anybody stupid enough to get within arm's reach. The cop that gets out of the squad car yells for the guy to get on the ground and put his hands behind his back, you know, like how they do with everybody, only the guy doesn't listen. He goes straight for the cop. The cop backs up a couple steps and pulls out his gun, all the time yelling for the guy to get on the ground.

The guy gets to within about five feet and the cop just unloads on him. Hits him three times in the chest, Jimmy's mom says. The fourth round goes wild and cracks off the sidewalk almost catching a bystander. This guy just keeps coming, Jimmy's mom says, and gets his hands around the cop's throat. She tells us how the guy leans in and bites the cops nose right off his face then rips his throat out right there in the street. By now everybody is losing their shit. Jimmy's mom says the store manager told everybody to get into the storage room and lock the door, he was gonna call more cops, but Jimmy's mom took off out the back door instead and hauled ass home. By then we had seen a couple of news reports about crazy people doing the same kind of shit. TV said it was some new drug that people were overdosing on, but we knew better. Fat lot of good it did us... We grabbed our arsenal from Jimmy's room, jumped in his car, and drove downtown. When we got there it was total chaos. It looked like riot footage only in real life. People were running everywhere, cars were on fire, buildings were on fire. It was crazy. We jumped out of the car looking for some zombies to tangle with. It didn't take long. A gang of them in police uniforms came out of an alley. We jumped on them. Stupid. Jimmy swings his big old sword and buries it the collar bone of one them then cant get the damn thing out again. He's jerking the handle trying to get the blade out and the whole thing snaps in half. Mitch starts in with his throwing knives, even manages to land a couple of hits. One of them right into the eye of one of the zombies. Mitch lets out this little victory cheer then turns to me to celebrate his first kill, only the thing doesn't go down. Mitch looks confused. We hear Jimmy scream and turn around just in time to see him get dragged down under three of them, still trying to get his machete out of the hip holster it was in. Mitch pulls a hatchet out of his belt and buries it in the skull of the one closing in on him. The zombie goes slack and falls to the ground. Mitch puts a boot on the back of its head and levers the blade back out.

While that was happening, I spotted one of the dead cops' revolvers laying on the ground. Score! I grabbed it up and came around bringing the gun up in an arc as I spun. Must have looked so badass right then. The only problem is that before that, I had never fired a gun before. I always figured it would be like in the movies and the comic books, you know, just aim and fire. I pulled the trigger six times, even though only the first two tries fired any bullets. Neither of them hit anything near as far as I could tell. I looked around for another gun or some bullets as me and Mitch tried to fall back to the car.

Mitch actually managed to take down two more zombies, but I could tell his arm was getting tired. The third one he got he had to kind of hack at before he could do enough damage and by then he couldn't get the blade back out of the thing's skull. He pulled a buck knife out of his pocket and flipped it open. We kept moving back to the car.

There were more of them in the street now. Mitch goes to stab one in the temple only I don't think he stabbed hard enough because the blade just sort of slid along the zombie's skull and peeled off a slice of its scalp. Mitch tried to stab again only the blade folded closed on his hand, cutting up three of his fingers bad, and he dropped the knife. The last of him I ever saw disappeared under half a dozen zombies as they dragged him to the ground and tore him apart. Actually, the last I saw of him was a chunk of meat and some intestines twirling through the air.

I turned and ran. I made it back to the car completely out of breath and not moving much faster than the dead that chased me. I pulled the door shut just as one of them made a grab for my shirt, taking off three of its fingers in the process. They landed in my lap with a little plop-plop-plop sound. That's when I threw up, the first time anyway.

I sat there for at least an hour crying, smelling like puke, trying to make sense of what just happened. Zombies surrounded the car. Not many, just a handful of them bumping and thudding on windows. All at once it became real. This wasn't some stupid video game or a movie I could put on pause so I could go take a leak and not miss the really gory parts. It was all the really gory parts. And I wasn't the super hero I always thought I was. I had gained all this knowledge over a decade and a half from movies, TV, books, comics… Surprisingly, they weren't that far off the mark when it came to what the Z-pocalypse would look like, except for that running bullshit. Yet here I was, completely mentally fucked, crying like a baby and uselessly waiting for somebody else to come and save me.

I don't remember how long I sat there with my eyes closed and blubbering. By the time I looked up there was only one zombie left. The others had either gone off after easier prey or had just gotten bored and wandered off. I started the car and tried to think of where the hell I could go. Back home? No way. I couldn't think about answering all my mom's questions and nagging and shit. I knew enough to stay away from the obvious places, Army base outside town, police station, hospital, church. These were always the first places people went when the shit hit the fan, and large groups of people were bad news in this scenario. I didn't have a bugout location. I never thought I would actually need one. Like I said, Mitch and Jimmy and I always figured we would save the day.

"Fuck it," I said to the walking corpse smashing its head into the windshield. I put the car in Drive and headed south. I figured I would pick up the interstate and head east to the coast. Then I would steal a boat, a big one, and head out into the ocean. I figured it was as good a plan as any at that moment. The longer I drove, the worse the roads got. After three hours, and maybe 10 miles on the highway, I got off and stuck to back roads. The going wasn't much quicker, but at least I wasn't going to get stuck in some giant clusterfuck traffic jam.

It took a few days, okay more like a week, to get to the East Coast. I remember being amazed at how quick everything went to shit. I guess people were too busy dealing with zombies to worry about some dude driving a piece of shit Corolla, so nobody messed with me. I saw some big groups of dead but I always managed to make my way around them. One time, I had to go through them. That was scary as shit and I almost got bogged down. I guess I would have been fucked, but I got away.

I was somewhere in South Carolina, damned if I knew where, when I saw the Atlantic. I started north figuring it would only be a matter of time before I found a boat. Truth be told, it didn't take long to find a marina full of big assed yachts. A lot of the spots were empty, like other people had already had my idea and had taken off. I got out of the car and headed toward the lines of boats slowly bobbing in the water. I hadn't bothered to try and find a weapon or anything. I moved down the first row and onto the closest yacht. Looking back, I have no idea what I was thinking. I had never even been to the beach, let alone on a boat, let alone driven one. Do you drive a boat? That doesn't sound right to me for some reason… Anyway, I found the steering wheel and realized you needed a key to start one of these things. I rooted around the little room trying to find keys, but no dice. A little voice in my head, the same one that used to tell me how bad ass I would be in a zombie attack, told me to try hotwiring the damn thing. Like that was an option. I climbed back outside and jumped down to the dock. I climbed into the next boat and immediately heard moaning coming from below the deck. I turned around and jumped off almost breaking an ankle in the process. I climbed into the third boat and as my head cleared the rail, I heard a shotgun rack. I froze.

"Ge' thFUCK off m' boat!" came a very drunk, but still authoritative voice.

"Please! Don't shoot!" I cried. "I'm just trying to... Trying to..." Trying to what, exactly? Steal a boat so I can run away from the undead? That sounded pretty stupid in my head. Besides, this guy had to know what was going on. "I just need someplace safe." Did I just say that? Jeez.

"Z'not safe here," the voice waivered, "S'prolly not safe anywhere." Then a laugh that was almost soaked in gin. "M'wifes downstairs. She's dead. But then again, she aint!" Again, the laugh.

I started to climb back down slowly not wanting to hear, or smell, this guy anymore. I wandered to another boat, but I heard moaning inside as soon as I put my foot on the deck, so that one was out. The next boat I tried was clear, but the cabin door was locked. I tried kicking the door in, a trick I had always thought would work just like TV. It didn't. I thought I was going to break my damn foot and the door barely budged. I tried another and another and another boat. Finally, I found one with the door unlocked. I climbed into the driver's seat or captain's chair or whatever you call it and I realized, I had no fucking clue how to drive a boat. There wasn't a gas pedal. No brake pedal either. There was a wheel at least, and after a minute or two I figured out the throttle. I pushed the big, red starter button and heard the engine chug to life somewhere under and behind me. I pulled back on the throttle and the engine roared a little louder. The boat started to slide backward and I relaxed a little. Then, it started to strain. I heard creaking wood as I pulled back more on the throttle. The engine whined higher and then I heard a snap and the crack of boards. I hadn't untied the big ropes from the dock. A big metal thing the rope was tied to, I think it's called a cleat, torn off the side of the boat, leaving a gaping hole in the side. I knew enough to know you don't take a boat out into deep water with a big, fucking hole in it.

I punched the steering wheel in frustration. This as supposed to be easier than this. I don't know why I thought that, but I did. I jumped from the boat to the dock as it drifted further away. I landed on the ankle I hurt trying to kick the other door in and a bolt of pain shot up my leg. I hobbled back to my car, now almost out of gas, climbed behind the wheel, and started to cry. I cried like a little bitch. And for a long time, too. This was bullshit! I had seen all the movies, read all the comics. My friends and I used to talk about how cool a zombie apocalypse would be. How we would ride around on motorcycles, fighting zombies and other assorted bad guys, maybe find some babes who would be so grateful for us saving them that they would be as sexually explorative as all the women on the internet. And yet here I was, stuck in a car, crying like a girl.

After that it gets kind of blurry. I know I drove north, otherwise I never would have found the flyer. I don't remember ever stopping for gas or to sleep, or if I ran into anybody, undead or otherwise. I remember crossing into New Jersey though. I drove over some big assed bridge that was almost completely clogged with cars. Halfway across, I had to abandon my car. As I moved on foot, zombies threw themselves at the, thankfully, closed windows of a lot of the cars. When I made it to the other side I found another car. Not right away, I had to walk a long time to find one that wasn't blocked in. That was some scary shit, too. You can outrun a zombie pretty easy, but if there is a group of them it's pretty unnerving.

I found a pretty sweet Camaro, but it was a stick shift. I finally landed a beat-to-shit, old pick-up truck.

The driver was half in, half out of the cab. I snuck up slowly just in case he wasn't, you know, all the way dead. I threw a rock at his head and when he didn't move, I figured I was in the clear. He had a piece of paper in his hand with a map on it. I figured maybe he was a Prepper and this was his stash. Why not? That kind of shit happened all the time in movies. What I saw instead was some outfit claiming to be a safe haven. Sure, my ass, I thought. They were either already dead, or they were luring people into some kind of cannibal trap. Damn thing looked like it was drawn by a four-year-old with some stubby crayons. The map wouldn't do any good anyway, I had no idea where I was. I crumbled it into a ball and threw it on the floor of the truck.

I climbed behind the wheel, turned the key still in the ignition and just started driving in the direction the truck was already pointed. Turns out, that was the first really smart thing I had done since this all started.

22

Ian

I walked in on Ken as he was firing up another computer. The look of frustration and dejection on his face damn near broke my heart. We knew when we headed out how big of a long shot this was, but now that it was right in my face, I couldn't help but think about the risks we took and the men we lost, all apparently for nothing.

"This is bullshit," Ken exclaimed as he caught my eye, "Everything is password protected. So far, I've been able to get into a couple HR files, but that's about it."

I tried to be consoling, "Maybe we can start with the paper files? Might be something in there…"

"Whatever. It's better than staring at a Windows login screen wondering why the fuck I thought this would ever work."

He moved to the carts stacked high with patient charts, picked the first one up and began to flip through it. "Vital signs, med lists, physical exam note, no labs results, no progress notes… Wait," his face contorted in concentration, "This is interesting. I think they were intentionally infecting some of these people."

"What?!" I exclaimed. "What the fuck do you mean, they were infecting people?! Like there weren't enough people getting infected the old-fashioned way!"

Ken raised a hand to calm me down, or just to get me to shut up so he could concentrate. He picked up another chart, flipped through it until he found what he was looking for, then another and another. After a while, he had a pile of them spread out in front of him all turned to some graph that made no sense to me, but seemed to interest the hell out of him. "Without any real context, this doesn't get me anywhere, but at least it's a start. First, they had no idea what the hell caused all this. It wasn't a virus or a bacteria or even a parasite, at least any that we knew about. Second, yes, they were exposing uninfected people to the pathogen in order to determine the vector, how the disease was transferred. Third, this had been going for at least a year. See this chart here, it's at least 18 months old"

That last part got me. I couldn't believe that. That the government I had worked for, given my life to, that I had watched my buddies die for, knew about this and didn't tell its people. Then again, as soon as the thought crossed my mind, I dismissed it as naïve like any other normal adult would. Didn't make me any less pissed off, though.

"Look, this is all really preliminary stuff. I need to go through what I've got here. I'll worry about the computer data later. Can you see if there are any other charts around? Maybe on one of the other floors? I don't want to risk a run in with those people again, but I really need more to go on."

"No sweat. I'm going to leave a couple of guys here with you. I'll take Ranger and scout out the other floors. I think I still remember my way around. Radio if there's trouble."

Ken had already waved me off and had his face stuck in

another chart. I guess this wasn't an entire waste after all.

23

Ken

I really had no idea what to make of most of what I found in those charts. A ton of inconsistent test results, they weren't even running the same panels on every patient. With no context, graphing titers and chem series were more than pointless, it was frustrating. The only thing I knew for sure is that the CDC had been running tests on infected patients since at least a year before the outbreak. If the notes I found were at all accurate, Patient Zero was sent to them from a hospital in Georgia. He was a John Doe that had been brought in by local police after he went insane and attacked a group of high school students on a field trip in the woods. The police that arrived on scene each emptied their service revolvers into the assailant and only succeeded in subduing him when all four grabbed and handcuffed him.

The attending physician at Georgia Methodist pronounced the patient dead after physical examination of his extensive wounds and a complete lack of any discernable vital signs. I imagine the fact that, though deceased, the man remained aggressive and violent, was why the CDC was contacted. I still haven't located John Doe's chart, but I'm not sure it will hold any magical keys anyway.

Out of the hundred or so charts I have been poring through, I have located Ian's as well as the charts of four other individuals who seemed to share his immunity. The research team here was no closer to an understanding of what caused the infection, let alone why certain people were immune, than when they first brought Patient Zero/John Doe through their basement doors. Each research lead kept their own notes, some extensively so, and none of them could agree on anything. That's part of the problem that existed, I'd seen it a hundred times myself. Virologist always see viruses, microbiologists see bacteria, mycologists see fungus. Sort of like what Ian calls training scars, only for scientists.

There were still too many missing pieces for me to make any conjecture, but this was at least a starting point. The two big questions were what had caused all this, and what the cure could be. Figuring out why Ian and, apparently, so many others were immune would go a long way to answering the second question, provided we could also answer the first. That would likely take a lot more data than what I had here. Even then, I could spend the rest of my life sifting through old charts and research notes and still not make any headway. I decided against getting pessimistic too early. Best just to focus on what was in front of me and let the big shit take care of itself.

24

Amy

The sound of Mick being attacked will haunt me for the rest of my life, however long that life ends up being. The horde engulfed the truck as soon as we crashed. Wedging myself between the seats and pulling all of our gear over myself and Zoe worked to save the two of us, but Mick had been left out in the open as they burst through the passenger window. He let out a single, panicked scream and then it was over. It wasn't his death howl that got to me, it was the never-ending feasting on his body with nowhere to escape to. Time stopped having meaning as an eternity of carnage rolled in.

Thank God that Zoe remained unconscious for it. It was my burden to carry. I was the one that left him to the wolves, and I would have to be the one to relive that moment many times in my mind. That is not the kind of memory a young girl should have burned into her psyche. The feast lasted longer than any nightmare should, and then it went quiet. The wave of dead had receded and was back to rolling across the landscape, destroying everything in its path.

The tears flowed hot and salty down my cheeks, until I

finally fell into the deep sleep that I had prayed so hard for hours before. There was no sense of urgency to see if Mick had reanimated or been devoured whole. There would be no rush to do anything, even chase after Garett and Emma. I was desperate for them to be alive, but losing Mick had pulled a dark veil over my eyes, one which was strangely familiar and oddly comfortable. This time, finding my way back to the place where hope lived seemed impossible. I could put one foot in front of another for Zoe, but she was right. What was the point?

When I awoke, I realized that my worst fear had begun loudly announcing itself. Mick was struggling to get out of the truck, but being a mindless eating machine had left him unable to think his way out of a wet paper bag, let alone a metal and glass prison. I was hoping that something would draw his attention in the direction of whatever opening the zombies had used to get to him and he would follow it right out of our lives forever. Instead, our long string of bad luck continued and I was forced to find a weapon with which to end Mick's zombie afterlife.

I was wedged so tightly between the seats that it would take a fair amount of movement just to get my hands free to explore the area around me. I worried that would alert Mick to our hiding spot and end with all three of us joining the ranks of the undead. Every movement was executed with bated breath and slow precision. My fingers crawled along the zippers of the bags that acted as the only barrier between us and a gruesome death. Without the luxury of sight, I had to unzip each bag and blindly feel my way around the contents. Three down and I had found nothing of any value. Just as I was about to give up and accept that we were all meant to die here, my hand landed on a cold, metal savior.

Metal fabric shears had just the right weight and overall size to crack through the skull without all the extra swing and effort that so many of our other weapons required. My mind walked through the steps I would need to take to uncover myself and spring forward with enough momentum to bury the shears in their intended target. Like a jack in box, I sprung, and while I had been poised to land the perfect kill shot, I hadn't anticipated another zombie being in Mick's place.

I was so startled that I almost missed my chance. I had forgotten that Mick was immune, like myself. So much time had passed and so many people had turned in front of our eyes that I had missed the most obvious outcome. Mick wouldn't be cursed with transformation, and neither would I. Our deaths would likely be messy and horrible, but they would be final, and there was a certain comfort in that.

With renewed hope, I buried the shears deep into the head of the zombie that was still feasting on Mick's lifeless body. I reached up, opened the door, and rolled them both out onto the ground. I kicked the zombie's still body until my foot ached, then slumped over Mick's body and had one final cry. I had loved him. We may only have been brought together because of the end of the world, and he may have not been my type before, but he was a good man and he didn't deserve to die like that.

I pulled a sheet out of the cab and covered his body. There was no way I would be able to give him a proper burial but I could still show him some respect. It was time to move out and see if Zoe and I could find the teenagers. With a little bit of searching, I was able to find a hatchback that had a half a tank of gas and no significant damage. It was ugly as sin, however, and looked like hitting a pebble might cause it to collapse into a pile of rust.

Within an hour, all of our supplies had been transferred to the passenger seat of the hatchback, which left room for a makeshift sleeping area in the back. I piled pillows and blankets in to make Zoe as comfortable as possible as she rested off her injuries. I wasn't ready to face the possibility that she may never wake up again. For that moment, I needed to continue to act as if she was going to be fine. When I moved her from the truck to the hatchback, I was sure I heard her groan. Maybe that meant something. Maybe it didn't.

I took it slow as I made my way out of town. As I rounded the corner back towards the highway we had come in on, I got a clear look at the damage the horde had caused to our caravan. Most of the vehicles that were in front of our truck had stayed right in their original place in the line, unable to break free once they were overtaken. Some had opted for staying in their cars and died in their hiding places. Others had taken the more proactive approach, and had tried to make a stand against the undead.

They never stood a chance, and their mangled bodies littered the ground as evidence. I felt nothing as I drove past, nothing except pity. They never really stood a chance against the reality of this new world. As a group, they had failed to elect a leader that they could put their trust in. By putting off the simple task of choosing someone to lead, something most groups had established in the very beginning, they had sealed their fate. Mick had died because of their incompetence. I lost the one person I had felt safe with, and for that I was unable to forgive their mistakes.

Zoe rolled over and let out a deep sigh. The bottle neck opened back up and I was able to get the hatchback out on the open road. I drove for hours hoping to see a sign or anything that would lead me to the teenagers, but the world was a chaotic place and I had no way of contacting them. Eventually, after driving around for hours and seeing no signs of life anywhere, I made the decision that we needed to head towards the sanctuary on the flyer. If they were still alive, that's where they would go.

I turned the rusty little car around and hit the gas with a bit more enthusiasm. With minimal breaks and, hopefully, some better luck than we'd had in the past few days, we could reach the sanctuary in a little over a week. It would just be a matter of pushing the gas pedal down more often than the brake and, once there, waiting patiently for Garett and Emma. Last time I saw them, they were alive and driving away. Mick and I taught them well, so I had to hope that they were capable of making it there on their own.

25

Garett

Emma and I waited on the rooftop for a week. Twice, we saw cars in the distance, but one quick look through our binoculars took away any hope that it was Aunt Amy, Mick and Zoe. The air was crisp at night and it was getting colder much too quickly to wait much longer for them. While I enjoyed the alone time with Emma, I missed my sister. Since we lost Hannah, I made sure to check in with Zoe every few hours. This separation was the longest we'd had since the outbreak, and each hour made me more antsy to find them.

"They may still be with the group," Emma said when she realized that I had been staring off into nothing again.

"Maybe, but I really hope not. I mean," I stumbled across my words. "Of course, I hope they're alive, just not with that group. They managed to kill a bunch of their own people in that last disastrous maneuver. Everyone knows that you always leave a way out. They were so hell bent on stopping in every town to grab as much as they could that they forgot what we were supposed to be doing."

"That's why greed is one of the sins. My mom always said

that the deadly sins would get you every time. My uncle was a gambler and he lost everything. Eventually, he lost his life, too. He lost money that he couldn't pay back to the wrong kind of guys. They just threw his body out in the desert." She had only started to share about her family this last week.

"I had a great aunt that had to be taken out of her house with a forklift after she died, so I think your mom was on to something. People think stuff like that's funny, but in the end, it's really just sad," I said.

"Yeah," she said, her face turning serious. "People can be cruel."

I cupped her face with my hands as I spoke, "I will never be cruel to you, Emma. I'll spend my whole life trying to make you happy in this fucked up world. You can always count on me to be there for you. I would die for you. You know that, right?"

Tears streamed down her cheeks. "Don't you do that. I don't want you to die for me. If it comes down to it, I want you to live for me. Our time here is short, no matter what. There's no way we get to grow old together anymore. But we can be together now. We can live every moment like some old ridiculous cliché. We can live like there's no tomorrow."

"I love you, Emma," I said as I pulled her body close to mine.

She fit me like we were two pieces carved out of the same chunk of wood. Her breath raised her chest against mine, and my entire body went hot. "I love you, too." She mouthed into my chest.

"Tomorrow, we leave. Okay?" She nodded against my chest. "It would be too easy to get lazy and stay here until we're forced to run. I would like to leave a place because it's our own choice for once. Sound alright to you?"

"What about your family?" She asked.

"Our family," I corrected her. "They'll probably spend some time looking for us, but eventually they'll head for the place in New Jersey. We're very close now. I think it's time to just head there and wait for them to show up. Aunt Amy's right about one thing. The cold is coming, and you and I are not ready for that. We need to get to where there are other people and shelter."

"I wish we could stay here forever, just you and me," she sighed.

"I know. Me, too." But we both knew there were a million reasons why that was a bad idea, so there was no point patronizing her by explaining them. Everyone thought Emma was dumb, but she was actually very intelligent. She was also painfully shy and only opened up to people when she felt safe. Lately, she was having a difficult time feeling safe.

"I want to sleep out under the stars tonight. We won't be able to do that for much longer. You want to help me drag out the air mattress?" She asked, breaking the silence.

"In a few minutes. I just want to sit here for another minute or two. Hopefully, we won't be alone much longer. This may be the last time we get to do this."

"You know we can do so much more since we're alone." She ran her hand up my thigh as she gently kissed my ear. "You know, since this might be our last chance."

The last sentence was a hot whisper in my ear that sent electric shockwaves through my body. How I could have been so dense as to have missed that she was ready to be with me was one of the great mysteries of life. The air mattress seemed to appear out of thin air, but it more likely was moved with the enthusiasm only a teenage virgin can muster.

Before I knew it, we were stripped bare and tangled under the night sky. We were surrounded by death and fear. Hate ruled the day, and bullies tried to take things that weren't theirs. But there, under the moon, we lay exposed to the world, safe for the moment and in love. It was a moment that wouldn't last but, while it did, it was perfection. Afterwards, as she lay in my arms, sleeping from exhaustion, I swore I would die for her regardless of what she said.

26

Reverend Mathis

After crossing the bridge and returning to level ground, I was elated, as was the rest of the group. We reveled in that victory for the next few miles. It seemed that our pace had even quickened despite the hunger and fatigue. Daniel said we should start looking for more vehicles and some of the hardier men headed off to find them. I saw some of them even clapping each other on the back and laughing as they went. The women crowded around the children as they usually did, preening and protective. They spit cleaned foreheads and smoothed mussed hair as best they could. They smiled genuinely as they told the children that it wouldn't be much farther now.

Someone rummaged through a discarded knapsack a produced a few chocolate bars. These were passed around the group and it seemed that everyone got at least a small square of the treat.

"Not quite loaves and fishes, but I'll take it," one of the men said as he handed me my share.

I laughed and nodded, "I could go for something a little closer to the wedding at Cana myself."

He returned my laugh. "Water into wine, right?"

I nodded again and smiled what was probably my first genuine smile in a long time. Daniel had moved off away from the group again, but I didn't want to bother him and risk destroying the lightened mood of the group. So instead, I sat down on the curb next to a gutter and savored my morsel of chocolate. The town around us looked almost peaceful, as if an apocalypse hadn't befallen the world. I wondered just then, if it was the whole world. I had been so insulated in my church, that I rarely ever watched the news. I had no idea if this plague was localized to North America, the United States, or even just the East Coast. I chuckled at my own foolishness.

Daniel eventually came around to where I was and hunkered next to me.

"This place is quiet, Rev. I've had some guys poking around here and there while we've been resting and they tell me the place is empty."

"Safe?" I asked.

Daniel nodded. "Maybe we should take a good, long look at where we're standing. There are more than a few good buildings here, bricks and cinder block. There's a fresh water lake a quarter mile north and woods for miles all around. Maybe we forget about this," he pulled the crumpled, torn flyer from his pocket, "and we set up shop here. I'll bet there's even a church around here somewhere."

"Do you think it will be okay with the size of that, that swarm only a few miles away?"

"You saw them Rev. They were just milling around. Almost like they'd have stayed there forever if we hadn't come along. I'm thinking once we set a perimeter here, you send a handful of fast runners back the way we came and have them lure that herd south. Have them go for a few miles, then turn east and make their way back without being seen. The zombies will keep going until they hit the Florida swamps, for all I know."

"We'll have to find something to eat. Why don't we stay the night? We'll let the group decide in the morning."

Daniel agreed and walked off toward a group of men. I saw him explain something to them and point to a few of the buildings. They split off in three small groups, presumably to find food.

They returned a short time later with duffels full of canned goods and armloads of firewood. Daniel built a fire in the alley between two brick storefronts as cans and bottles of water were passed around. The Townies traded one another for the various cans of tuna or fruit cocktail and broke off into small conversations. A few thanked Daniel for the work he did on the bridge and for finding them food. He shook hands and joked with them. Maybe they were finally beginning to re-accept him into the group. I thought about bringing up his idea to make a new home in this place but decided against it. I feared it might be a long discussion and as the sun dipped behind the buildings and the evening chill crept in, I figured that the Townies would prefer to snug down and get some much-needed rest. If it were meant to be, it could wait until morning.

Conversations went on as the sun set and one by one, or two by two if you will, the Townies moved into one of the buildings and made their beds for the night. Daniel and I were the last to remain outside. The night had indeed grown chilly. Daniel doused the remains of the fire and we went inside. I saw Daniel give one last look around before entering as if taking it all in. It may have only been my imagination, but I believe I saw a look of hope, and maybe even satisfaction on his face. I was asleep almost as soon as my head hit the pile of rags that served as my pillow.

I was shocked awake by the sound of shattering glass, then a scream. Then another. The third was followed by a hissing sound as of steam escaping a radiator. The room quickly filled with a cloud of acrid burning smoke.

"Gas! Gas! Gas!" Daniel screamed as he waved his arms over his head in what almost looked like a weight lifting gesture.

Those closest to the door threw them open and rushed outside. There waiting were several large men who began clubbing the first few who staggered through. Daniel clapped a t-shirt to the front of his face with one hand and grabbed for his rifle with the other. The Townies stumbled about, not knowing what to do. My own instincts fought within me, wanting to go out to the clean air, but knowing that brutal hands awaited me there. After I could hold my breath no longer, it came rushing from me in a violent exhale. I tried to breathe in, but my lungs refused the acid cloud that filled the room to every corner. My eyes stung and any exposed skin burned. The men waited just outside the doorway as they had no masks. One by one, the Townies, unable to bear the gas any longer, would rush out the door. Each was met with the butt of a rifle. Their limp body was caught as it fell and carried off. I couldn't see where. And I did not want to.

Daniel's rifle, at least I believe it was his, who else would have had the fortitude to put up any semblance of a fight at that point, began to crack in the darkness. I saw one of the men outside fall backward, his hands flying to his neck and a red spray arcing into the air. The other men jumped back as Daniel fired several more times. Another window at the back of the room shattered inward and the barrel of a shotgun poked through. The boom was deafening and the flash temporarily blinded me. I heard someone scream behind me. As I turned the shotgun exploded again and then again. I caught site of someone, I couldn't tell who through the haze, immediately to my left just as the buck shot hit them. Her chest disintegrated and she dropped to the floor. She didn't even have time to gasp.

Gunfire rang out all around me then. My only thought was for the children. I called out names, but only received screams in return. I began to crawl through the burning fog trying to find any of the children. The shotgun went off again just a few feet behind me. My ears rang and I felt crumbles of cinder block fall across my back. I hurried forward not caring if the shot was meant for me. If it was, I would already be dead. Again, I called out to the children by name and again I got no response. I heard Daniel yelling orders to the men that remained alive. He was telling them to break the remaining windows to let out the gas while he fired alternately through the doorway and back through the windows.

The men outside continued to grab anyone that went out, yet made no attempt to enter the building. Daniel hadn't succeeded in taking any more of them down. I heard one of the men outside call, "How many?" Another answered, "Fourteen." Then I heard a loud cat call whistle and the gunfire from the windows ceased. I heard the slam of a sliding metal door, as of one on a van and an engine fired up. I looked over to Daniel, a knowing and terrified looking passed over his face and he bolted to the doorway. He dropped to one knee and began firing out toward a target I could not see.

Tires peeled and a few shots were fired back. I ran to the door in time to see several vehicles' taillights disappearing around a corner. Several of the Townies had broken from the building and tried to give chase on foot but no avail. Our attackers were gone. It was then that the significance of the "Fourteen" hit me. Fourteen was the number of our camp that they had taken. Taken to where and to do what with, I could only imagine. As the shock of the realization sunk into me, I heard the moans and crying from those that were left coming from behind me. I turned and went back inside, the poison had almost cleared now. There were bodies strewn all over the floor, blood and vomit pooled around mangled figures. Some of the bodies were far too small. Still, I grieved less for those whose husks remained in this room than for those who had been kidnapped.

Anyone who was able had made their way out to the alley where only a few hours ago, Daniel and I had contemplating building a home for ourselves here. There was no way that would happen now.

"We have to go after them." It was John, one of the few men left. "There's no telling what those bastards are going to do to them."

Murmurs of agreement circulated among the group along with "They took the children" and "probably cannibals" and "make them pay".

Daniel answered in a whisper, "We can't go after them."

There were shocked gasps in response.

John gathered up his large frame and glared at Daniel. "Why the fuck not?! We're just supposed to let those, those sons of bitches take our... take our..." He broke down in sobs. I passed a glance back toward the remaining children and saw that John's son was not among them.

Daniel cast his eyes downward. "There's no way. We don't

know where they went, how many of them there are, how many guns they have. None of it. For all we know, they'll cut us down right around that corner right there." He pointed toward the intersection where the trucks were last seen. "There aren't enough of us left to put up much of a fight," he added bluntly.

With that reality put so plainly, many of the group began to wail openly. Daniel was likely right. There were maybe two dozen of us left. To have our number cut down so swiftly shook me. I turned and went back into the building, raising a hand to those who moved to follow me.

I knelt in the blood beside one of the bodies. I rolled the small, eleven-year-old husk onto its back, crossed its arms over its chest and closed the blue eyes that a day before had still held an innocence that this world would likely never see again. I said a prayer to the God I wasn't sure listened to me anymore that He might take mercy on these souls and on those that had been taken. 'Give them peace, Lord,' I thought, 'At least let their deaths be swift.'

I moved around the room offering what may have been considered Last Rights to each corpse that was once a member of our family. I wept without tears over every one of them. I have no idea how long this took, but when I had finished I rose from my knees, my pants soaked and dripping with blood and gore, to find Daniel in the doorway.

"We gotta move, Rev. Either those motherfuckers will be back or, more likely, all that noise will have drawn the crowd we avoided earlier. The Townies are ready. We were just waiting for you."

I nodded and walked, slump shouldered and exhausted out to the group. As I passed Daniel, I turned and said, "Burn it down, Daniel. Not one of these should be cursed to rise again."

Daniel then nodded in return. "Way ahead of you." He had set a five-gallon gasoline can just inside the doorway. "I'll wait until you guys are on your way, then I'll light this place and catch up to you."

We had no choice then. At that moment, our only hope lay with the faint promise held by the flyer.

27

Max and Rocky

I wish I had found someone like Jeremy from the beginning. He might be a grown up, but he never really acted like he was or treated me like I wasn't. I don't know. It's just so much easier with him. Daniel and the Rev were fine for a while, but they were always fighting about something. They reminded me of my friend Randy's parents. His parents started bickering and having small fights while we were playing. I think they were trying to hide it from us. Some people think kids are stupid.

Anyway, they'd start with these small fights, hiding inside, thinking we don't know what is going on. But over time, those fights got bigger and harder to hide. It always made my stomach feel weird when they would fight. I felt bad for my friend. Sometimes I would bring him back to my house for a sleep over. Sometimes, though, I would just run back home to hide from all that craziness.

My mom would shake her head and ask my dad, "Why don't they just get divorced, already?" I didn't really know what that meant until one day I went to play at Randy's house and he told me his dad didn't live there anymore. Things were quiet there after that. We got to play more and have fun, except for when Randy went to his dad's place. Then I would just have to wait for him to get back.

I wonder if Daniel and the Rev ever got divorced. They should have. It would have been much quieter and I would have had a lot less stomach aches. It didn't matter anymore, though. I was heading to that fort that everyone seems to want to get to. Problem is I can't decide if I feel like being around a huge group of people again. What if they are as bad at getting along as Daniel and the Rev were? I feel like it might be a better idea for me and Rocky to just keep doing our thing.

I kind of like hanging around with Jeremy, especially if he keeps puking all the time. That is so funny. The sound he made still makes me laugh every time I think about it. Rocky seems to like him better than any other person we have met out here so far, and I trust Rocky when it comes to judging people. He seems to know when someone is up to no good. We spent most of our time hopping from car to car, making our way down some random back roads in New Jersey. Eventually, we found ourselves at what I thought to be a pretty strange sight until Jeremy told me it was actually a tourist spot.

Thompson's Family Farm looked more like an amusement park than a working farm. It had fields, sure, but it also had rides and playground equipment. There were signs with prices for each activity they offered. Many of them were things my dad had to pay people to help with, not the other way around. They also had a splash pad and a petting zoo. The biggest building towards the front had huge signs advertising pies and jellies, all the things my mom would make during the harvest. The weirdest part, though, was that none of the buildings seemed to be very damaged. As we walked through, I started to feel like we were being watched.

"Jeremy? Do you feel like somebody is…"

He cut me off before I could finish my question.

"Just keep walking like you aren't suspicious, but yeah, I think there's someone else here. It's way too nice. What does Rocky think?"

Rocky's ears perked up at the sound of his name. He sniffed at the air and gave a sharp yip. He smelled someone, and they weren't dead. He didn't seem very concerned, though. Normally, he would bite at my rear until I moved fast enough out of the area where he sensed danger. There may be someone nearby, but Rocky didn't think they were a problem. That was, until the bullet ricocheted off a metal sign near Jeremy's head. Jeremy dove onto the ground but Rocky turned and began barking at the building that was advertising the pies.

He bolted towards the front door and slammed into it with his full weight. I had never seen Rocky so mad, not in the entire time since we had left our own farm. He had never acted that way before. It was almost like the shot had sent him over the edge. I pulled myself up off the ground and ran towards him.

"No, Kid! No! Get back here!" Jeremy screamed at me as I ran. "The dog can take care of himself!"

"I have no one else left! Rocky! Come on, boy! They just want us to leave," I begged as I ran towards my seemingly rabid dog.

When my hand touched Rocky's back, he instantly calmed down. He sat at full attention with each of his hairs standing on end and an almost soundless growl that came from deep inside his chest.

"Stay where you are or we'll shoot all three of you. And kid, you better figure out how to calm that dog down before we come out. Do you understand?" A voice from inside the building ordered.

"Yes, sir," I answered. "Calm down, Rocky. If they were going to shoot us, they would have done it when we were out in the open." I scratched his head as I explained to him, even though I wasn't totally sure it was the truth.

He backed down some more, curling up against my feet with his eyes closed. I think he was playing possum. There was a series of knocks sent back and forth between the top and bottom floors. So, they had signal, too. Nice to know.

As the door creaked open, I saw that a gun was pointed at my forehead.

"Kid, just listen to them and everything will be fine, okay?" Jeremy's voice shook as he tried his best to convince me, even though he didn't totally believe it himself.

I wasn't stupid, though. I had made it a long time on my own, well, with Rocky, but you know what I mean. I knew to do what they said, at least until what they said didn't make sense anymore. But by that time, I would find a way out. That was always my plan when I came upon strangers. If I couldn't hide quick enough, I would play the 'dumb kid' part. That's what they all thought I was anyway.

I looked over at Jeremy and he winked. I guess he didn't think I was stupid. Maybe, he was smarter than I thought. The owner of the gun stepped out from behind the door. She was a girl, and she was right around my age. She quickly looked me up and down and then, keeping the gun pointed at me with one hand, stretched her other hand out in front of Rocky's face.

"I know you're faking it, pup," she said.

His eyes popped open and he sniffed at her fingers. Then he did something that most people would consider rude and licked her fingers as if they were covered in food, all while his tail went crazy.

"I knew peanut butter would do the trick," she said as I stared at her, mouth on the floor. "You need to get him to go back out to your dad and then we can talk. Any weapons you have need to be dropped on the ground right now."

"Whatever you say," Jeremy replied before I had a chance. "Here, boy."

Rocky stood up and marched his way over to Jeremy like a good little soldier. He sat and kept his eye on the girl but I knew it was only because he was hoping that she might have more peanut butter for him to munch on. She had figured out his kryptonite. I sat down 'crisscross applesauce' style and waited for the group to figure out what they were going to do with us. Jeremy got up off his belly, and sat right next to me.

"Stay there now," she said as she pointed the gun at his head for the first time. "Papa, we all clear?" She yelled up to the window of the pie building. "You two alone?" She asked as she kicked Jeremy in the leg.

"Yup. Just me, the kid, and the dog. We're just passing through," he answered.

"They say they're alone. What do you think, Papa?" She yelled up again.

"I'll be down in a minute. Don't let them move," her father answered.

"You two better not move. I'll shoot you right in the head. I used to be afraid to do stuff like that, but now..." She stopped for a minute. "Now, I'll put one right between your eyes."

A man walked through the front door of the pie house, but he couldn't have been her Dad. He seemed much too old. His hair was all crazy and grey, and he had a beard that was a lot like Santa Clause's.

"What's your name, son?" He asked.

"Jeremy. This is Max, and that's Rocky." He motioned towards Rocky, who had decided upon seeing the old man that he could lay down and relax.

"What's your business here, Jeremy?"

"We were just passing through, sir. Max and I want to get to a place called Batsto. You ever heard of it?"

"Bet you found one of those dang flyers. I don't know why so many of you youngsters are willing to trust a piece of paper you found on the ground."

"We don't really have anywhere else to go. Seemed as good as any place," Jeremy explained.

"That's a pretty stupid reason to go somewhere. What happens if you bring this boy right into a trap?" He pointed his finger at me accusingly as he asked.

"What if it isn't a trap and the kid can finally get a decent night's sleep?" Jeremy asked.

The old man glared at Jeremy for a moment before he finally said, "You promise not to cause us any trouble, you can get a decent night's sleep here."

Rocky's ears shot up and started to twitch.

"He hears something, mister. We need to get inside. Can we move, please? I don't want to get eaten out here."

"You see something, Jim?" The old man called out over his shoulder.

"Twenty or so coming down the road. All dead," a voice answered.

"We'll take this conversation to the barn, but if any of you try anything funny, it will be the end of you," he warned us.

We marched into what the old man referred to as a barn.

While it was shaped like a barn, it wasn't what any real farmer would call a barn. It had been a store at one time, with rows of cash registers and signs for pies and fruit and different things to eat. All the food was long gone, though. It had all been replaced with supplies that had been neatly stacked everywhere. Each different type of item seemed to have a separate pile. It reminded me of the thrift store at my old church, except that it was all things you would need to fight zombies and stay warm.

"Don't you go getting any ideas, boy. I see you checking out our stash. We worked hard to get all of this stuff together, and we sure aren't going to have some newcomers come in and take everything we worked so hard to get." The old man gave me a small shove to keep me moving forward.

"It just reminds me of my church's swap," I said in a small voice.

Rocky slid his head under my hand and helped me keep my cool while we followed the girl up a set of stairs that was hidden behind a fake wall. That was the point when I started to get a bit worried. It wasn't usually a good thing when someone brought you to a hidden place. I had seen enough movies to know that it almost always ended badly.

When we reached the top of the stairs, we found three closed doors. We were herded through the last one into a room at the end of the hall, which was empty except for a few mattresses on the floor. It looked like we were going to be spending the night here, whether we liked it or not. The door slammed behind us and the lock clicked, then the footsteps headed back in the other direction. Jeremy had his face pressed up against the slit of a window. It was not big enough for either of us to escape, but we could see far enough down the road to watch the group of dead that were headed towards the farm.

"I think we're going to be waiting around for a little while, Max. You tired?"

"Not really, we haven't been walking that long today. I am pretty hungry, though. What do we have left in the pack?"

"I can't believe they didn't take our bags from us, just our weapons. They're either really stupid, or they're not as big and bad as they are trying to make us think. You okay with cold canned whatever in a sauce of whatever?" He asked with a smirk.

"Man, when you put it that way, it sounds delicious!"

"That's why I like you, kid, always the optimist," he said as he smiled.

"I don't know what that means, but thanks."

"It means, well, who cares what it means. You and I should figure out our plan before they get back. I think we should tell them I am not your dad if it comes up again. I don't want them to think that they can use hurting you to get to me. I like you and all, but not the way a dad loves his kids, you know? That could be a liability."

"Okay," I said as I started to chow down on the can of cat food that Jeremy had handed me. "It would be nice if they weren't jerks. I could really use a meal that doesn't consist of cat food."

"Me too, kid. Maybe we'll get lucky and they'll be alright. I just want to be ready in case they aren't." Jeremy was shoveling some kind of food into his mouth using three fingers as a scoop. I should be grossed out because he was slurping up something we used to think was too disgusting to eat. Now, it just seemed normal to pop open a can of "mystery meat", as he called it, and munch away.

"Rocky doesn't seem too worried," I said as I pointed at my dog, who was snoring away on one of the mattresses.

"Yeah, but he did just get a peanut butter bribe. I don't know if we can trust his judgement," Jeremy laughed.

"Good point," I said as I put the empty can down. I popped open a bottle of water and laid down next to Rocky. "Maybe I'll just close my eyes for a minute."

"Not a bad idea. I'll keep watch. If I see anything, you'll be the first to know."

I must have been more tired than I thought. As soon as my head landed on Rocky's soft fur, it was lights out.

28

Jeremy

I didn't want to tell the kid, but I wasn't very confident that this group was made up of what most would consider normal people. What kind of host locks you away in a cell? And aside from that, who has a room with an exterior lock ready to go? That was some bizarre shit right there. I guess it could be useful in situations like this, you know, as a quarantine area or to keep new people that you didn't trust in a controlled space until you figured out what to do with them, but the idea of it gave me the heebie-jeebies.

It was nice to see the two of them sleep for real for once, though. They normally slept in shifts. They trusted me, I guess, but not enough for Rocky to let me be the only one watching the boy. He would lay next to him, but every little noise would make his ears twitch. Who knew it would take being held prisoner to make the two of them feel secure enough to fall into a snoring, drooling pile?

The only window in the room was three or four inches wide and about a foot and a half tall. It wasn't really a window, but more like a slit in the wall that had been covered with glass. After I finished my latest meal of what could barely be considered food, I stood beside it and peered out to see what was happening on the ground level. From there, I could get a better headcount of the people in the group. There were eight outside that I could see but the girl wasn't with them, so that made nine. There may have been more, but for such a large group, they were good at being quiet.

We hadn't heard any of them when we first walked onto the farm. For such a large group to be so disciplined that they could remain completely silent and out of sight as the newcomers are surrounded is quite an amazing feat. I wondered if they had sent the girl out so we would be thrown off guard. She seemed capable enough. Maybe the point was to show us even the less threatening members of their group were willing to put one between our eyes.

I watched through the slit as the group took down a small pack of zombies in what looked like a well-choreographed dance. They didn't use a single gun, which was smart. No need to make all that noise. All it would do is drive more of the dead to our location, and no one wanted that. They worked together with a variety of farm tools, some of which were being used as-is, while others had been modified to keep the dead as far away as possible, skewering them through the brains.

Once all of the dead had been put down, two group members threw them into wagon being pulled by a horse and drove off with them. You had to admire their commitment to cleanliness. Honestly, I don't think I had seen a place that was as well maintained as this one had been since way back before the outbreak. Most people were worried about surviving, not a manicured lawn.

The people that were left behind huddled up and began what

looked like a heated discussion. A few of them gestured toward the window, leading me to believe we were most likely the stars of the conversation, which made sense. If they didn't like leaving a mess lying around, they definitely couldn't have uninvited guests mucking up their world. It appeared that they had come to a consensus. The group broke apart and everyone headed back in whatever direction they had originally come from. I was jealous of how they seemed to work like a well-oiled machine. So far, besides Max and Rocky, every group that I managed to fall in with had been a disaster.

I backed away from the window and sat on the second mattress with my back against the wall. I figured they would be coming up soon enough to tell us what the jury had decided. There had been nothing about the way the group had broken up that led me to believe that they would be hostile, so I let Max sleep. Rocky could decide for himself if he needed to be up or not. I wasn't about to act like I had better instincts than an animal. Especially not when every decision I'd made in my life so far had proven that I did not.

There were three quick raps on the door. Maybe they weren't going to kill us. People don't normally bother with pleasantries when they're planning to execute you. The same old man who had put us in the room walked back in. He looked over and saw that Max and Rocky were asleep.

"Come down stairs with me. We'll let the boy sleep. Same arrangement as before. Try something, and it'll be the last thing you do."

"Deal," I said. I stood up in the least confrontational way I could think of but I'm sure it ended up just looking awkward.

The door on the left opened silently, no creaky hinges here. Papa seemed to run a tight ship. He motioned for me to take a seat across from him as he sat in one of the most luxurious office chairs I had ever seen. My chair, on the other hand, was not meant to be occupied for extended periods of time. While it wasn't exactly uncomfortable, it wasn't very comfortable either. It did match the décor perfectly, however. Each detail had been thoughtfully considered while furnishing this room.

"The others are split about what we should do with you. That means that it comes down to me, since this place was mine before the zombies started coming around."

"Fair enough," I replied.

"I'm not sure about you. The kid would be fine to stay, but you're a grown man. There's a lot to be considered there. I already know you were nice enough to let the kid travel with you. Seems fed, and happy enough."

"How'd you know he isn't mine?" I asked, a bit surprised.

"You didn't call him by his name. You called him 'kid'. Plus, the dog listens to him, not you. If they were your family, the dog would see you as the alpha. It doesn't."

"You're an observant man," was all I could think to say in response.

"Meticulous and observant. I let people stay here, but there are rules. And those rules are non-negotiable. I know you had a plan to go to Batsto. Do you even know what it is?"

"I lived in Jersey on and off a few times in my life. It's some state park or something, right? I think a friend dragged me there for a fall festival or something. Best candied pecans I ever had." My mouth watered as I remembered them.

"The commonly held belief is that the military or government fled there, but does that make any sense to you, boy?" His stare was intimidating, like it had been practiced for a lifetime. "Why would they go to some park in the woods when there are more than a few bases around here? There are much better places to ride the end of the world out than a park that holds festivals," he spat out.

"That's kind of rich…" It slipped out of my mouth before I could stop it.

"Excuse me? Something wrong with a farm?" He asked angrily.

"Not necessarily, but sir, your farm is more like a playground compared…"

The sound of his fists hitting the desk cut me off mid-sentence and made me jump. "You think being a farmer is easy? Farmers were going broke until we came up with the idea of agritourism! Each year we added more things for people to do, more stuff to buy. It was a way of surviving, just like now. We always find a way to survive!"

"I'm sorry, I didn't mean to insult you. It's a beautiful farm. I was just thinking before you came to get me that it was the nicest looking place we've seen since the rest of the world went to hell. Forgive me, I meant no insult." I hoped that appealing to his ego would get him back on my side.

"What is it that you want, son? Are you trying to find a place to live or are you still just trying to stay alive? Because the people that live here are setting up a place to live. This is our home, and everyone here plays a part in making it safer and better. What skills do you have?" His mood flipped like a switch, and I wasn't sure I liked that at all.

"Not much, really. I kind of drifted along. I always thought there would be more time for me to figure out what I was going to be or do. I didn't expect the world to end," I answered honestly.

"That's no good. What a waste. You're far too old for that

nonsense. I'm not sure I want to keep someone around that I'm going to have to train. I'll need to think on it. I'm going to have one of the ladies bring dinner up to the two of you. The dog is going to need to go out to relieve himself. We'll take him. No need for either of you to leave the room. I'll have my decision for you by the morning."

He waved me away as I began to stand so that I could make my way back to the room. I was fairly certain I could rest easy for the evening, which would be a nice change of pace. He also said we would be getting a meal, and, unless it was two cans of cold animal chow, that would be a treat. His decision meant very little to me, unless he decided to kill us, of course. I, for one, would not like to spend whatever time I had left on God's green earth taking orders from someone's controlling grandfather.

I let Max sleep until the food arrived. The woman who left the trays and locked the door also took Rocky with her. "I promise I'll bring him right back," she said to Max as she hooked a collar and leash on him.

"He doesn't like to wear a leash, ma'am."

"It's just to keep him safe. He'll be okay," she said as she led him out the door and clicked the lock into place once more.

The room was suddenly filled with the aroma of the heavens above. The trays were not a disappointment. It was a shame their leader was, or the food may have been enough to convince me to stay. There were fresh zucchini and squash, cooked in what smelled like honest-to-god butter, with scrambled eggs and a roll. And the drink. Oh, the drink was what pushed it over the edge to heavenly. It was apple cider, fresh from the farm's orchard. And if that wasn't enough to send me into a flavor coma, they had placed a piece of apple pie on the tray, too.

Max looked down at his tray with tears in his eyes. "I think we should stay."

"That's just the food talking."

"Probably. I still think we should stay," he said before he shoveled a bite of pie into his mouth.

"Don't eat too fast. You should try to enjoy it."

He chewed slowly for a minute. "If we stay, we could eat like this every meal."

"You're allowed to make your own decisions, kid. I knew you might not stick around when we teamed up, but I just want you to know what I think before you make your decision. I had a talk with Papa while you were asleep, and he is all over the map, Max. He seems like the kind of guy that lets people believe they're involved in deciding things, but really it's all him. And if you don't do it his way, you're out, or worse. I just don't want to see you guys get hurt." My food was getting cold but I knew he needed to hear it.

"Let's worry about it after dinner," he said.

We were just about finished when the woman brought Rocky back up to our room. "I'll take those trays for you. Did you enjoy your meal?" She asked with a smile.

Her smile was so genuine, I wanted to push down that bad feeling that I had, but it just wouldn't stop nagging at me. As soon as she closed the door, we heard that familiar sound of the lock being engaged. The three of us took the opportunity of being locked behind several doors on the second story of a building with bellies filled with warm and delicious food to drift off to a full night's sleep.

Once morning came, my body almost didn't accept the fact that we would no longer be lying in an actual bed and resting.

The door was unlocked and in walked a giant of a man who, in the time before zombies, must have been either a bouncer at a bar or a railroad spike driver. I am fairly certain that the latter occupation hadn't been available in over a hundred years, but he would have definitely been qualified. He carried with him two towels and a basket of toiletries.

"I was sent to tell you to wash up before breakfast," he said in a baritone that would make Barry White jealous.

"Thank you. Come on, Max. We're finally going to stop smelling like a dirty sock."

That perked him up. He scooped his bag up and bounced down the stairs behind the man, Rocky following quickly behind. I've never seen a kid his age that excited to get cleaned up. Most spend their lives in pursuit of the level of filth that we live with on a daily basis. We were led out of the barn and down a long hill to a second house. The two-story white farmhouse looked like it came straight out of a movie. Unlike the store and play areas, that house was exactly what you thought of when you pictured an all-American farm.

There were people wandering around with purpose every-where on the property. They looked like the human equivalent of bees in a hive. Everyone had a job, and no one needed to be directed as to how to do it. They worked together in perfect harmony. I wished it was something I could handle being a part of but, even though I longed for it, I knew my personality couldn't handle the rigid rules that I would have to follow to stay in the good graces of those in charge. That was never really something I was good at doing.

"The bathroom is inside. Once you're done, follow the smells to find the kitchen. They'll load you up with your morning meal," he said as he dismissed us.

"They seem nice," Max said as he bounded through the front door, leaving Rocky to stand guard on the wrap-around front porch while he waited for us to return.

I turned back and saw two small children run up with chow for him. It was going to be difficult to convince either of them to want to leave at this rate. I meant it when I said that they could stay or go as they pleased, but I needed to know that they were going to be alright. Maybe I should just mind my own business and let the kid stay in what looked like a safe and happy place. My hang-ups weren't his issue.

There was warm water in the shower. I was floored by the luxuries that this group had managed to set themselves up with. Papa was right. I wished I knew his real name because I hated to sound like a grown man with a daddy complex, but he was right. They weren't just surviving, they were thriving. I toweled off and resigned myself to the fact that I would be eating my last good meal for a while. After I finished drying off, I looked around for my clothes, only to find them missing. They had been replaced by a pile of freshly laundered clothes that were unbelievably close to the right size.

Max was already down in the kitchen when I finished up. He was almost unrecognizable. "Miss Claire gave me a haircut. She said no respectable boy could walk around looking like a scrub-bum." He said, running his fingers through his now significantly shorter locks.

"Now he can see what's going on without his hair getting in the way. I think you look very handsome, Max. I used to be a hairdresser in my previous life. I make sure everyone around here looks presentable. That and I work the breakfast shift. I'm just glad they let me stay here," she said as she piled up a plate of warm food for me. "I should give you a quick cut, too.

If you think the shower made you feel like a human again, wait until you get a trim."

"Thank you, ma'am. That would be wonderful. Can I eat while you cut? I am starving and I don't want them to have to wait for me."

"Sure thing, sweetie." She looked ecstatic as she pulled her shears out and headed in my direction.

I tried to savor each bite but my stomach was having none of it. In the end, all I did was pick at it. Max, on the other hand, shoveled the food into his mouth at lightning speed. He was eager to start his day as a member of this new group. I knew then that I had lost the two best traveling buddies I had been blessed enough to find on this crazy journey.

Papa was waiting at the bottom of the porch steps as we left the farmhouse. It was a surreal feeling, walking out into the real world again. The farmhouse was a bubble in time, a place that held our lost civilization in a secret world of hot showers and warm food.

"I see Nancy gave you both a good haircut. Good, good. Well, boys, you passed the test last night. Anyone who can spend a night in the locked cell and not cause any trouble gets the offer to be one of us. You can stay, but know, you'll have to pull your weight around here. Max, you'll be just fine, a good farm boy like you," he said as he watched Max's eyes grow wide in surprise. "Yeah, I got you pegged. You're too comfortable around here to be anything else. Jeremy, you have some work to do, but we can make it work as long as you're willing to do what we ask."

"I need to talk to Max, sir," I said as I turned to Max.

"That's what I thought," he said, turning to walk away. "Real shame you don't think you can make it work, but I understand.

You can stock up on some supplies before you go. We have more than enough." He stopped and turned his head back to look at me. "I hope you find whatever it is that you're looking for out there."

"Thank you. By the way, you never told me your name."

"Mr. Thompson, but everyone calls me Papa. Goodbye, son."

Max looked up at me with tears in his eyes. "You're leaving? Why? Can't you just hang around for a little while? Maybe it won't be too bad. Look," he said as he pointed at his dog, "even Rocky is happy!"

Rocky chased a stick far out into a field. A bunch of kids had taken a shine to him. There would never be a shortage of belly rubs or neck scratches. It was easy to see the appeal for the two of them.

"I need to go now, kid, or I never will."

"So what? Then you stay. Is that such a problem?" He argued.

"Don't make this harder. I'm going to miss you and the pup. You guys are the best people I've met so far, maybe ever. This just isn't my kind of place, but it is perfect for you and Rocky. Now I get to say I did something good in this crap world. I helped a kid find his real home."

"That's cheesy, and you're being stupid." He turned away from me.

"Probably, but that would be no different than before the zombies came. Look at me, Max. I want to say good bye for real. I am going to head to that Batsto place. If they really are the good guys, I will tell them you're all here. They might be able to find a way to send you word or something." It felt ridiculous as it left my mouth, but I needed to believe I could communicate after I left.

"Yeah, maybe," he whispered.

I whistled for Rocky and he came running over. With one last roll in the grass, I was able to say good bye. I brushed the dirt off as I stood up and then pulled Max into a hug.

"Stay cool, kid."

"You, too," he said, squeezing me as hard as his little body would allow. "If you change your mind, you can always come back."

I rustled his freshly cut hair and walked away. He didn't need to see the tear or two that fell from my face. With each step, I questioned my decision, but in the end I knew it was the right thing to do. The place from the flyer would torture my curious nature for the rest of my life if I didn't head there to see what it was. And who needed that kind of crazy hanging over their head for eternity?

About the Authors

Father of eight from the South Jersey Shore, Kris has always had a love for writing, horror and zombie fiction, and absurd, inappropriate humor. He co-wrote his first full-length novel, Aftershock, and now Breakdown with his wife Valerie. The two now live in the Pine Barrens with their pile of children and enough stockpiled Nerf weapons to take down an army of the undead.

While she mostly focuses on Horror, Valerie Lioudis is a multi-genre author who has been known to dabble in post apocalyptic, science fiction, and even metaphysical stories. The common thread with Valerie's work is her constant sarcasm, and love for bringing the unexpected to her readers. She loves the art of writing a short story, and has merged that with giving back to those in need. Many of the anthologies she is involved with donate their proceeds to groups near and dear to her. Two of the causes she is proud to say she has helped raise money for through writing are Veterans and Breast Cancer charities. She is an active member of the Reanimated Writers Facebook group, and can found there to answer any questions you may have about any of her work. Come join the horde, we would love to have you.

Follow Valerie on Facebook, Twitter, or Instagram.

For more stories in the Aftershock Zombie world, pick up a copy of Undead Worlds, or Undead Worlds 2 (release date October 16th, 2018) today and meet the character Avery.

Other Works

Zombies:

Aftershock (Book 1 in the Aftershock Zombie Series)
   Undead Worlds
   Undead Worlds 2 (Coming Soon)
   Tales From the Zombie Road: The Long Haul Anthology
   The Reanimated Rumble
   Treasured Chests

Novels and Short Story Collections:
   The Many Afterlives of John Robert Thompson
   From the Deep Dark

Non-Zombie Anthologies Featuring a Lioudis Story:
   Night Mares
   100 Word Drabbles
   Terrors Unimagined: An Anthology of the Supernatural and Horrific
   High Tech/Low Life: An Easytown Anthology
   Mad Like Me
   The End

Thank You

If you enjoyed this book, please take a few moments to write a review about it. It doesn't need to be long to make a difference, and we always love hearing what our readers think of the books we write. Thank you!